Rare Treasures from
GRIMM

Rare Treasures from
GRIMM

Fifteen little-known tales selected and translated by
RALPH MANHEIM

from *Grimms' Tales for Young and Old: The Complete Stories*
translated by Ralph Manheim

PAINTINGS BY ERIK BLEGVAD

Doubleday & Company, Inc.
Garden City, New York

The stories contained in this book previously appeared in the book *Grimms' Tales for Young and Old: The Complete Stories*. Translation Copyright © 1977 by Ralph Manheim. Published by Doubleday & Company, Inc.

Library of Congress Cataloging in Publication Data

Grimm, Jakob Ludwig Karl, 1785–1863.
  Rare treasures from Grimm.

  Selections from a translation of Kinder- und Haus-
märchen by J. Grimm and W. Grimm.
    CONTENTS: Darling Roland.—Thousandfurs.—The donkey
lettuce.—[etc.]
    1. Fairy tales, German. [1. Fairy tales. 2. Folk-
lore—Germany] I. Grimm, Wilhelm Karl, 1786–1859, joint
author. II. Manheim, Ralph. III. Blegvad, Erik.
IV. Title.
PZ8.G882Rar   398.2′1′0943
ISBN: 0-385-14548-9 Trade
ISBN: 0-385-14549-7 Prebound
Library of Congress Catalog Card Number 80–2350

Contents

List of Illustrations

Preface

A beautiful princess has left home and is wandering through the forest. She has taken three dresses with her, one as golden as the sun, one as silvery as the moon, and one as glittering as the stars, all hidden in a nutshell, and she is so well covered by a cloak made from a thousand different kinds of fur that she looks like an animal . . .

A woman has three daughters, one with one eye, one with two eyes, one with three eyes. "As Two-eyes looked no different from other people, her sisters hated her. . . ."

A little girl's six brothers have been turned into swans, and the only way she can save them is to go without speaking or laughing for six years and sew them six little shirts out of starflowers . . .

A king has a great forest, apparently a fine place to hunt in, but the huntsmen who venture into it never come back. After many years, a brave young huntsman discovers that it's all the fault of a "wild man," who has been lying at the bottom of a pool . . .

A young man who has been robbed of his treasures by witchcraft discovers two miraculous varieties of lettuce, one that will turn a human being into a donkey and one that will turn him (or her) back into a human again. His troubles, of course, are over . . .

After getting the better of the wicked witch, a young girl and her true love find themselves far out in the country. "I'll go home to my father," says the young man, "and arrange for the wedding." "I'll stay here and wait for you," says the girl. "And to keep from being recognized, I'll turn myself into a red stone." Whereupon she waits and waits . . .

A father sends his son away to get educated, but all he learns after three years of schooling is the languages of dogs, birds and frogs. His father is disgusted, but with this intellectual baggage the son goes far, very far indeed . . .

These startling happenings are related in a matter-of-fact tone that seems to make no distinction between real and unreal, between miracles and the most common facts of life. The young lady with the thousand furs, for instance, owes her success in life as much to the delicious bread soup she makes for the king as to the extraordinary dresses she carries about in her nutshell. And that is why, in translating Grimms' *Tales*, I thought it important to avoid fairy-tale style and to use everyday language.

In addition to being beautiful in themselves, I feel that Erik Blegvad's illustrations have captured just the right balance between reality and fantasy.

This book is made up of tales which, I believe, will be unfamiliar to many readers. Although there is great charm in reading and rereading the better-known stories—such as "Hansel and Gretel," "Snow White" and "The Musicians of Bremen"—there is a special delight in discovering new tales and seeing them for the first time with a fresh eye. This is the experience I had in making these translations, and the one I hope you will enjoy with this book.

—Ralph Manheim

Rare Treasures from
GRIMM

Thousandfurs

There was once a king, whose wife had golden hair and was so beautiful that there was none on earth to compare with her. It so happened that she fell ill and when she felt she was about to die, she called the king and said: "If you decide to marry after my death, don't take anyone who isn't as beautiful as I am and who hasn't got golden hair like mine. You must promise me that." When the king had promised, she closed her eyes and died.

For a long while the king was inconsolable and had no thought of taking a second wife. At length his councilors said: "There's no help for it; the king must marry, for we must have a queen." Messengers were sent far and wide to look for a bride in every way as beautiful as the dead queen. But in the whole world there was none to be found, and even if one had been found she would not have had such golden hair. So they came back empty-handed.

Now the king had a daughter who was every as bit as beautiful as her dead mother, and she had the same golden hair. One day when she had grown up, the king looked at her and saw that she resembled his dead wife in every way. He fell passionately in love with her and said to his councilors: "I am going to marry my daughter, for she is the living image of my dead wife, and I shall never find another like her." When they heard that, the councilors were aghast. "A father cannot marry his daughter," they said. "God forbids it. No good can come of sin, and the whole kingdom would be dragged down to perdition with you."

The daughter was even more horrified when she heard of her father's decision, but she still hoped to dissuade him. She said to him: "Before I consent to your wish I must have three dresses, one as golden as the sun, one as silvery as the moon, and one as glittering as the stars. In addition, you must give me a cloak made of a thousand kinds of fur, a snippet of which must be taken from every animal in your kingdom." "He can't possibly get me all that," she thought, "and maybe trying will distract him from his wicked plan." But the king was not to be discouraged. The most accomplished maidens in his kingdom were made to weave the dresses, one as golden as the sun, one as silvery as the moon, and one as glittering as the stars, and his hunters were sent out to capture all the animals in the kingdom and take a snippet of fur from each one. When the cloak of a thousand furs was ready, the king spread it out in front of her and said: "The wedding will be celebrated tomorrow."

When the king's daughter saw there was no hope of changing her father's mind, she decided to run away. That night when the whole palace was asleep, she got up and took three things from among her treasures: a gold ring, a little golden spinning wheel, and a golden bobbin. Then she put her three dresses—the sun dress, the moon dress, and the star dress—into a nutshell, wrapped herself in her cloak of a thousand furs, and blackened her face and hands with soot. After commending herself to God, she slipped out of the palace, and walked all night until she came to a large forest. By that time she was tired, so she crawled into a hollow tree and fell asleep.

They put her into the wagon and drove her to the royal palace.

The sun rose and she went on sleeping, and she was still asleep when the sun was high. Now it so happened that the king to whom this forest belonged was out hunting. When his dogs came to the tree they sniffed and ran around it and barked. The king said to his hunters: "Go and see what sort of animal is hiding there." The hunters did his bidding. After a while they came back and said: "There's a strange animal in that tree, we've never seen anything like it. It has a thousand different kinds of fur, and it's lying there fast asleep." The king said: "See if you can catch it alive, then tie it up, put it in the wagon, and we'll take it home with us."

When the hunters grabbed hold of the girl, she woke up in terror and cried out: "I'm a poor child, abandoned by my father and mother. Have pity on me and take me home with you." "Thousandfurs," they said, "you'll be just right for the kitchen. Come with us, you can sweep up the ashes." And they put her into the wagon and drove her to the royal palace. There they settled her in a den under the stairs, where the daylight never entered, and said: "This will be your bedroom and living room, Thousandfurs." After that she was sent to the kitchen, where she was made to do all the nasty work, hauling wood and water, keeping up the fires, plucking fowls, cleaning vegetables, and sweeping up the ashes.

For a long while Thousandfurs led a wretched life. Ah, my fair princess, what's to become of you! But one day a ball was given at the palace, and she said to the cook: "Could I go up and watch for a little while? I'll stand outside the door." The cook replied: "Yes, why not? Just so you're back in half an hour to sweep up the ashes." She picked up her little oil lamp and went to her den, took off her fur cloak, and washed the soot from her face and hands, revealing her great beauty. Then she opened the nutshell and took out the dress that shone like the sun. As she walked up to the ballroom, all the courtiers stepped aside for her, for none of them recognized her and they thought she must be a king's daughter. The king came up to her, gave her his hand and danced with her, all the while thinking in his heart: "Never have my eyes beheld anyone so beautiful." When the dance was over, she curtseyed, and before the king knew it she had vanished, no one knew where. The guards who were posted outside the palace were called and questioned, but none had seen her.

She had run to her den, quickly taken her dress off, blackened her face and hands, and put on her fur cloak: she was Thousandfurs again. She went to the kitchen to do her work and sweep up the ashes, but the cook said: "Let that go until tomorrow, and make the king's soup instead, because I'd like to go up and look on for a while. But don't drop any hairs in it or you won't get any more to eat." The cook went upstairs and Thousandfurs made bread soup for the king as best she knew how. When it was done she brought her gold ring from her den and put it in the dish.

When the ball was over the king sent for his soup, and it tasted so good that he thought he had never eaten better. When he got to the bottom of the tureen, he saw a gold ring and couldn't imagine how it had got there. He sent for the cook, who was terrified and said to Thousandfurs: "You must have dropped a hair in the soup; if you have, you'll be beaten!" When he appeared before the king, the king asked him who had made the soup. The cook replied: "I did." "That's not true," said the king, "because it wasn't made in the usual way and it was much better." The cook said: "I have to admit I didn't make it. Thousandfurs made it." "Send her to me," said the king.

When Thousandfurs appeared before the king, he asked: "Who are you?" "I'm a poor child who's lost her father and mother." "What is your work in my palace?" he asked, and she replied: "I'm good for nothing but having boots thrown at my head." "And where did you get the ring that was in my soup?" She replied: "I don't know anything about any ring." So the king got nothing out of her and had to send her back to the kitchen.

Some time later there was another ball. Again Thousandfurs asked the cook for leave to look on. He replied: "Yes, but be back in half an hour to make the king the bread soup he's so fond of." She ran to her den, washed herself quickly, took the dress that was as silvery as the moon out of the nutshell, and put it on. When she went upstairs, she looked like a king's daughter. The king came up to her and was glad to see her again. A dance was just starting, so they danced together. When it was over, she vanished again so quickly the king couldn't see where she went. She ran down to her den, made herself into a furry animal again, and went to the kitchen to make bread soup. When the cook went upstairs, she took the little golden spinning wheel and put it in the tureen, and the soup was poured over it. Then the soup was brought to the king and he ate it. He liked it as well as he had the first time and he sent for the cook, who had to admit once again that Thousandfurs had made it. Again she appeared before the king, but again she said she was good for nothing but having boots thrown at her head and didn't know anything about any golden spinning wheel.

When the king gave a ball for the third time, it was just the same as before. The cook said: "Thousandfurs, you must be a witch. You always put something in the soup that makes the king like it better than my soup." But when she begged and pleaded, he let her go for the usual length of time. She put on the dress that glittered like the stars and stepped into the hall. Again the king danced with the beautiful girl and thought she had never been so beautiful. While they were dancing he slipped a gold ring on her finger without her noticing. He had given orders that the dance should last a long time. When it was over, he tried to hold on to her hands, but she tore herself loose and ran off into the crowd so quickly that she vanished before his eyes.

She ran as fast as she could to her den under the stairs, but as she had stayed too long, more than half an hour, she couldn't take off her beautiful dress. She just threw the fur cloak over it, and in her haste she didn't smear all her fingers with soot—one of them stayed white. She ran to the kitchen, made bread soup for the king, and when the cook went upstairs put the golden bobbin into it. When the king found the bobbin at the bottom, he sent for Thousandfurs. As she stood before him, he caught sight of her white finger and saw the ring he had slipped on it while they were dancing. Thereupon he seized her hand and held it fast. When she tried to tear herself away, her fur cloak opened a little, and he caught the glitter of her starry dress. He tore off her cloak, uncovering her golden hair, and there she stood in all her glory, unable to hide any longer. When she had washed the soot and ashes from her face, she was more beautiful than anyone who had ever been seen on earth. The king said: "You are my dearest bride. We shall never part." Then the wedding was celebrated and they lived happily until they died.

Darling Roland

There was once a woman who was a genuine witch and she had two daughters, an ugly, wicked one, whom she loved because she was her own, and a beautiful, good one, whom she hated because she was her stepdaughter. At one time the stepdaughter had a pretty apron. The other daughter liked it so much that she grew envious and said to her mother: "I must and will have that apron." "Hush, my child," said the old woman. "Have it you will. Your stepsister deserved to die long ago. Tonight when she's asleep I'll go and chop her head off. Just take care to lie on the inside of the bed and push her to the outside." The poor girl would have been lost if she hadn't been standing in the corner and heard every word they said. They didn't let her out of the house all day, and when it came time to go to bed the witch's daughter got in first so as to be on the inside. But when she had fallen asleep, her stepsister pushed her gently to the outer edge and took her place by the wall. In the dead of night the old woman came creeping in. In her right hand she held an ax and with her left hand she groped to make sure someone was lying on the outside. Then she gripped the ax in both hands and chopped her own child's head off.

When she had gone away, the girl got up and went to the house of her sweetheart, whose name was Roland, and knocked at the door. When he came out, she said: "Darling Roland, we must run away; my stepmother tried to kill me, but she killed her own daughter instead. When the sun comes up and she sees what she's done, we'll be lost." "All right," said Roland, "but you'd better take her magic wand first. Without it we'll never get away if she follows us." After taking the magic wand, she picked up her stepsister's head and let three drops of blood fall to the floor, one by the bed, one in the kitchen, and one on the stairs. Then she hurried away with her darling.

In the morning when the old witch got up, she wanted to give her daughter the apron and called her, but she didn't come. "Where are you?" the old woman called. "Here on the stairs. I'm sweeping," said the first drop of blood. The old woman went out, saw no one on the stairs, and called again: "Where are you?" "Here in the kitchen. I'm warming myself," said the second drop of blood. She went into the kitchen, but found no one and called once more: "Where are you?" "Here in bed. I'm sleeping," cried the third drop of blood. She went to the room and approached the bed. What did she see? Her own child bathed in blood; and she herself had cut her head off!

The witch flew into a rage and leaped to the window. She had the gift of seeing far into the distance and she saw her stepdaughter hurrying away with her darling Roland. "A lot of good that will do you!" she cried out. "You've gone a long way, but I'll catch you." She put on her seven-league boots that covered an hour's journey at each step, and overtook them in no time. But when the girl saw the old woman striding up, she took the magic wand and turned her darling Roland into a lake and herself into a duck swimming in the

She took the magic wand and turned her darling Roland into a lake and herself into a duck.

middle of the lake. The witch stood on the bank, tossed in crusts of bread, and did everything she could think of to lure the duck. But the duck didn't let herself be lured, and at nightfall the old woman had to give up and go home.

The girl and her darling Roland took back their natural forms and walked all night until daybreak. Then the girl turned herself into a beautiful flower growing in the middle of a bramblebush, and turned her darling Roland into a fiddler. In a little while the witch came striding up and said to the fiddler: "Dear fiddler, may I pick that lovely flower?" "Yes, of course," he replied. "And while you're doing it I'll play for you." She knew perfectly well who the flower was, and as she hurried into the bush in her eagerness to pick the flower, he began to play. Like it or not, she had to dance, for it was a magic tune. The faster he played the more she had to jump. The brambles ripped her clothes off, and cut and scratched her till she was all covered with blood. But he kept right on playing and she had to dance till she fell to the ground dead.

Once they were saved, Roland said: "Now I'll go home to my father and arrange for our wedding." "I'll stay here and wait for you," said the girl. "And to keep from being recognized I'll turn myself into a red stone." So Roland went away and the girl, who had turned herself into a red stone, stood in the field, waiting for her darling. When Roland got home, he fell into the clutches of another woman and forgot his sweetheart. The poor girl stood there for a long, long time, but when he didn't come back, she grew sad, turned herself into a flower, and said to herself, "If only someone would come along and trample me to death."

But it so happened that a shepherd who was minding his sheep in the field saw the flower. He thought it was so beautiful that he plucked it and took it home and put it in his cupboard. Then weird things started happening in the shepherd's hut. By the time he got up in the morning, all the housework had been done; the floor had been swept, the tables and benches dusted, a fire made in the hearth, and the water brought in; and when he came home at midday the table was set and a good meal was ready. All this puzzled him, for he never saw a living soul, and the hut was too small for anyone to hide in. Of course he was glad to be so well served, but after a while he began to feel frightened and went to a Wise Woman for advice. The Wise Woman said: "There's magic at the bottom of this. Look sharp when you wake up in the morning. If you see anything moving, no matter what, throw a white cloth over it. That will break the magic." The shepherd did as she had said, and the next morning, just as day was breaking, he saw the cupboard open and the flower come out. Quick as a flash he jumped out of bed and threw a white cloth over it. That broke the magic, and there stood a beautiful girl, who confessed that she had been the flower and kept house for him. Then she told him her story, and as he liked her he asked her to marry him, but she said no, because even if her darling Roland had forsaken her she meant to be faithful to him. But she promised to stay with the shepherd and go on keeping house for him.

The time came for Roland to be married, and in that country it was the custom that all the girls for miles around should attend the wedding and sing in honor of the bridal couple. When the faithful girl heard the news, she was so sad she thought her heart would break. She didn't want to go, but the others came and took her along. Every time she was supposed to sing, she kept stepping back, but in the end she was the only one left and she couldn't help herself. When she started her song and Roland heard her, he jumped up and said: "I know that voice. That's my true bride, I don't want the other." Everything he had forgotten, everything he had lost sight of, suddenly flowed back into his heart. The faithful girl was wedded to her darling Roland, her sorrow was ended, and her joy began.

The Donkey Lettuce

There was once a young hunter, who went to a blind in the forest. He was joyful and lighthearted, and as he strode along, whistling on a blade of grass, he met an ugly old crone, who spoke to him saying: "Good day, young hunter, you seem so happy and content, but as for me, I'm hungry and thirsty. Could you give me a few pennies?" The hunter felt sorry for the poor old woman, reached into his pocket, and gave her as much as he could afford. As he was starting off again, the old woman held him back, saying: "Listen to me, my dear young hunter. Because of your good heart I'm going to make you a present. Just keep on your way now, and in a little while you'll come to a tree with nine birds perched on it. They'll be holding a cloak in their claws and fighting over it. Take your gun and shoot into the midst of them. They'll drop the cloak, and one of the birds will be hit and fall down dead. Take the cloak. It's a wishing cloak. Once you throw it over your shoulders, you need only wish yourself somewhere, and there you'll be in a flash. And if you take the heart out of the dead bird and swallow it whole, you'll find a gold piece under your pillow each and every morning of your life."

The hunter thanked the Wise Woman, and thought to himself: "Those are fine things she's promised me. If only they come true."

When he had gone about a hundred paces, he heard a screeching and a squawking in the branches. He looked up and saw a whole flock of birds, all tearing at a piece of cloth with their beaks and claws, screaming and tugging and fighting as if each one wanted it all to himself. "Well, well," said the hunter. "This *is* strange. It's just as the old woman said." He took his gun, fired into the midst of the flock and sent the feathers flying. The birds scattered with loud cries, but one fell to the ground dead, and the cloak came fluttering down. The hunter did what the old woman had told him. He cut the bird open, found the heart and swallowed it whole. As for the cloak, he took it home with him.

When he woke up the next morning, he remembered the old woman's promise and looked under his pillow to see if she had told the truth. A shiny gold piece sparkled up at him, and the next day he found another, and another and another every time he got up in the morning. He soon had a large pile of gold, but in the end he thought: "What good is all this gold to me if I stay home? I think I'll go and see the world."

He took leave of his parents, slung his knapsack and his gun over his shoulders, and went out into the world. One day he passed through a dense forest, and in the open country at the end of it was a beautiful castle. An old woman and a lovely girl were standing at one of the windows, looking down. The old woman was a witch, and she said to the girl: "See that man coming out of the forest? He's got a wonderful treasure. We must relieve him of it, my dear, because we can make much better use of it than he ever could. This treasure of his is a bird's heart, and thanks to it he finds a gold piece under his pillow every morning."

But after the first few bites he had a very strange feeling and something told him he had changed completely.

16

She went on to tell the girl how the hunter had come by his treasure and what she must do to get it. In the end the witch threatened her and said with flaming eyes: "You'll be sorry if you don't obey me." When the hunter came closer, he saw the girl and said to himself: "I've been wandering about for so long. I've got plenty of money, so why wouldn't I stop and rest in this beautiful castle?" But the real reason was that he had cast an eye on the lovely girl.

He went into the castle, where he was well received and entertained. Soon he was so much in love with the witch's daughter that he could think of nothing else. He lived by the light of her eyes and gladly did whatever she asked. One day the old woman said: "We must get that bird's heart. He won't even notice it's missing." They brewed up a potion and when it was ready the old witch poured it into a cup. The girl gave it to the hunter, saying: "My dearest, now you must drink my health." He took the cup, drank the potion, and vomited up the bird's heart. The girl carried it off in secret and then swallowed it herself, for that was what the old witch wanted. From then on the hunter found no more gold under his pillow. Instead, it was under the girl's pillow, and the old witch took it. But he was so madly in love that he had no other thought than to while away the time with the girl.

Then the old witch said: "Now we've got the bird's heart, but we must also take his wishing cloak." The girl replied: "Couldn't we let the poor man keep his cloak, now that he has lost his wealth?" At that the old witch grew angry and said: "A cloak like that is a wonderful thing. There aren't many like it in the world, and I must and will have it." She told the girl what to do and said she'd be sorry if she didn't. So the girl did as her mother told her, and stood at the window looking out over the countryside as though she were very sad. "Why are you standing there looking so sad?" the hunter asked her. "Oh, my dearest," she said, "over there across the valley lies the Garnet Mountain, where the precious stones grow. I long for them so. But who can get at them? Only the birds that fly through the air. A human being, never. That's why I'm so sad." "If that's all you've got to be sad about," said the hunter, "it won't take me long to cheer you up." Taking her under his cloak, he wished himself on the Garnet Mountain, and one-two-three they were both there. The precious stones that sparkled all about them were a joy to behold. When they had gathered up the most beautiful and costly of them, the old witch cast a spell that made the hunter drowsy. He said to the girl: "Let's sit down and rest awhile. I'm so tired I'm falling off my feet." They sat down and, resting his head in her lap, he fell asleep. While he slept, she took the cloak from his shoulders, threw it over her own, picked up the garnets and precious stones, and wished herself back home.

When the hunter had had his sleep out and woke up, he saw that his loved one had betrayed him and left him alone on the wild mountain. "Oh," he sighed. "Oh, what treachery there is in the world!" He sat there grieving, and didn't know what to do. The mountain belonged to some great ferocious giants, who made their home on it, and it wasn't long before he saw three of them coming. He lay down as though he had fallen into a deep sleep. When the giants caught sight of him, the first one prodded him with his foot and said: "Who's this earthworm lying here gazing at his inner thoughts?" The second said: "Step on him, crush the life out of him." But the third said contemptuously: "Why bother? Let him live. He can't stay here, and if he climbs to the summit the clouds will pick him up and carry him away." With that they left him, but the hunter had heard what they said, and as soon as they had gone, he stood up and climbed to the summit. When he had sat there awhile, a cloud came drifting along, picked him up and carried him away. For some time it floated around the sky, then it settled on a big walled kitchen garden, and he landed gently among the vegetables.

He looked around and said to himself: "If only I had something to eat! I'm so hungry I'd have a hard time going anywhere. But here I see no apples or pears or fruit of any kind, nothing but vegetables." Finally he thought: "In a pinch I could eat some of that lettuce. I doubt if it tastes very good, but it ought to be refreshing." So he picked out a nice-looking head and bit into it, but after the first few bites he had a very strange feeling and something told him he had changed completely. He had four legs, an enormous head, and two long ears, and he saw to his horror that he had turned into a donkey. But since he was still very hungry and since, now that he was a donkey, the fresh, juicy lettuce was very much to his taste, he ate and ate. Finally he came to a bed of a different kind of lettuce, and no sooner had he eaten a few leaves of it than he felt himself changing again and his human form came back to him.

After that he lay down and slept away his weariness. When he woke up in the morning, he picked a head of the bad and a head of the good lettuce and thought: "This will help me to get my treasures back and to punish the treachery of those women." He put the salad in his knapsack, climbed the wall, and set out in search of his sweetheart's castle. After wandering around for a few days, he found it. Before going in, he dyed his face brown so his own mother wouldn't have known him. Then he went to the door and asked for a night's lodging, saying: "I'm too tired to go any farther." "Who are you, my friend?" asked the witch, "and what is your business?" "I'm the king's messenger," he replied. "The king sent me in search of the most delicious lettuce in the world. I was lucky enough to find it and I've got some with me, but the sun is so hot I'm afraid the tender leaves will wilt, and I don't know if I can carry it any farther."

When the old witch heard about the delicious lettuce, her mouth watered for it and she said: "Dear friend, let me taste your wonderful lettuce." "Why not?" he replied. "I've brought two heads, and

I'll give you one." He opened his knapsack and handed her the bad lettuce. The witch, who suspected nothing, was so eager to taste the strange new lettuce that she went to the kitchen herself to prepare it. When it was ready, she couldn't wait till it was on the table, took a few leaves and put them in her mouth. The moment she swallowed them she lost her human form, became a donkey, and ran out into the yard. Just then the servant came in, saw the lettuce all ready in the bowl and thought she'd serve it. She carried it to the table, but, as usual, she couldn't resist her desire to taste it. She ate a few leaves and the magic worked instantly: she too was turned into a donkey. The salad bowl fell to the floor and she ran out to join the old witch. Meanwhile the king's messenger was sitting with the lovely girl, and when no one came in with the lettuce, she too began to long for it. "I wonder what's become of that lettuce?" she said. "Aha!" thought the hunter. "It must have worked." And he said to her: "I'll go to the kitchen and see." When he got down to the kitchen, he saw the two donkeys running around in the yard and the lettuce lying on the floor. "So far so good," he said. "Those two have got what was coming to them." He picked up the rest of the lettuce leaves, put them in the bowl and took them to the girl. "I've brought you the delicacy myself," he said, "so you won't have to wait any longer." She ate some, and like the other two she became a donkey and ran out into the yard.

When the hunter had washed his face so that the donkey women could recognize him, he went out to the yard and said: "Now you're going to get what you deserve for your treachery." He fastened all three to a rope and drove them down the road till he came to a mill. He tapped on the window and the miller stuck his head out and asked him what he wanted. "I've got three ugly-tempered beasts here," he said, "and I'm good and sick of them. If you'll take them and feed them and treat them just as I tell you, I'll pay you whatever you ask." "Why not?" said the miller. "But how do you want me to treat them?" The hunter explained: "Beat the oldest (that was the witch) three times a day and feed her once. Beat the middle one (that was the servant) once a day and feed her three times. As for the youngest (that was the girl), feed her three times and don't beat her at all." For he couldn't find it in his heart to have the girl beaten. Then he went back to the castle, where he found everything he needed.

A few days later the miller came to him and said: "I'm sorry to tell you this, but the old donkey, the one that got beaten three times a day and fed only once, is dead. The other two have been getting fed three times a day and they're still alive, but they're so sad they can't be expected to last much longer." At that, the hunter took pity, forgot his anger, and told the miller to bring them back to the castle. As soon as they arrived, he gave them some of the good lettuce to eat, and they resumed their human form. The girl went down on her knees to him and said: "Oh, my dearest, forgive my wickedness, my mother made me do it. I didn't want to, for I love you with all my heart. Your wishing cloak is hanging in the cupboard and I'll take a vomitive to make me bring up the bird's heart." But he wouldn't let her do that. "Keep it," he said. "It makes no difference who has it, for I mean to take you as my trusted wife."

Then the wedding was held and they lived happily together until they died.

The Peasant's Clever Daughter

There was once a poor peasant who had no land, just a small house and an only daughter. One day his daughter said: "We ought to ask the king for a piece of newly cleared land." When the king heard how poor they were, he gave them a piece of grassland, which she and her father spaded, meaning to sow a little wheat and other grain. When they had almost finished spading their field, they found a mortar of pure gold. "Look here," said the father. "The king was kind enough to give us our field. Why not give him this mortar in return?" The daughter was dead against it. "Father," she said, "if we give him a mortar and no pestle, he'll want a pestle. We'd better keep quiet about it." But the father wouldn't listen. He brought the mortar to the king, said he had found it in his field, and asked if the king would accept it as a gift. After accepting the mortar, the king asked the peasant if he hadn't found anything else. "No," said the peasant. "What about the pestle?" said the king. "Bring me the pestle." The peasant said they hadn't found any pestle, but he might have been talking to the wall. He was thrown into prison and the king told him he'd stay there until he produced the pestle.

When the servants brought him his bread and water—that's what they give you in prison—they heard him sighing: "Oh, if I had only listened to my daughter! Oh, oh, if I had only listened to my daughter!" The servants went to the king and told him how the prisoner kept sighing: "Oh, if I had only listened to my daughter," and how he wouldn't eat and wouldn't drink. The king had the servants bring him the prisoner and asked him why he kept sighing: "If I had only listened to my daughter!" "What did your daughter tell you?" "Well, she told me not to give you the mortar, because if I did you'd want the pestle too." "If you have such a clever daughter, tell her to come and see me." So she appeared before the king, who asked her if she were really so clever, and said: "I'll tell you what. I've got a riddle for you. If you can guess the answer, I'll marry you." "I'll guess it," she said. "All right," said the king, "come to me not clothed, not naked, not riding, not walking, not on the road, not off the road. If you can do all that, I'll marry you."

She went home and took off all her clothes so then she was unclothed, sat down on a big fish net and wrapped it around her, so then she was not naked. Then she hired a donkey and tied the fish net to the donkey's tail, and the donkey dragged her along, which was neither riding nor walking. And the donkey had to drag her along the wagon track, so that only her big toe touched the ground and she was neither on the road nor off the road. When she came bumping along, the king said she had guessed the riddle and met all the requirements. He let her father out of prison, took her as his wife, and gave all the royal possessions into her care.

Some years passed, and then one day as the king was inspecting his troops, some peasants, who had been selling wood, stopped their wagons outside the palace. Some of the wagons were drawn by oxen and some by horses. One peasant had three horses, one of them foaled, and the foal ran off and lay down between two oxen that were harnessed to another peasant's wagon. The two peasants started

The foal ran off and lay down between two oxen.

to argue and fight, because the one with the oxen wanted to keep the foal and claimed the oxen had had it. The other peasant said no, his mare had had it, and it belonged to him. The dispute came before the king. His decision was that where the foal had lain there it should stay, and so it was given to the peasant with the oxen, who had no right to it. The other peasant went away weeping and wailing about his foal. But he had heard that the queen was kindhearted, because she came of a poor peasant family. So he went to her and asked if she could help him to get his foal back. "Yes," she said. "If you promise not to give me away, I'll tell you what to do. Tomorrow morning when the king goes out to inspect the guard, take a fish net, stand in the middle of the road where he has to pass, and pretend to be fishing. Shake out the net now and then as if it were full and go on fishing." And she also told him what to say when the king questioned him.

Next day the peasant stood there fishing on dry land. As the king was passing by, he saw him and sent his orderly to ask the fool what he was doing. "I'm fishing," was the answer. The orderly asked him how he could fish when there was no water. The peasant replied: "There's just as much chance of my catching fish on dry land as there is of an ox having a foal." The orderly took the man's answer back to the king, whereupon the king summoned the peasant. "You didn't think up that answer," he said. "Where did you get it? Tell me this minute." The peasant wouldn't tell him. "So help me," he said, "I thought of it myself." But they laid him down on a bundle of straw and beat him and tortured him until at last he confessed that the queen had given him the idea. When the king got home, he said to his wife: "Why have you played me false? I won't have you for my wife any longer, your time is up, go back to the peasant's hovel you came from."

But he granted her one mercy, leave to take the best and dearest thing she knew of with her. That would be her farewell present. "Yes, dear husband," she said. "If that is your command, I will obey it." She threw her arms around him and kissed him and asked him to drink a farewell glass with her. Thereupon she sent for a strong sleeping potion. The king took a deep draft, but she herself drank only a little. When he had fallen into a deep sleep, she called a servant and took a fine white sheet and wrapped it around the king. The servant carried him to a carriage that was waiting at the door and she drove him home to her little house, where she put him into her bed. He slept a day and a night without waking. When he finally woke up, he looked around and said: "Good God, where am I?" He called his servants, but there weren't any servants. At last his wife came to his bedside and said: "Dear king and husband, you told me to take what was best and dearest with me from the palace. Nothing is better or dearer in my eyes than you, so I took you with me." The king's eyes filled with tears. "Dearest wife," he said, "never again shall we part." He took her back to the royal palace and married her again, and I imagine they are still alive.

King Thrushbeard

A king had a daughter who was unequaled for beauty, but she was so proud and thought so much of herself that no suitor was good enough for her. She rejected one after another and to make matters worse poked fun at them. Once the king gave a great feast and invited all the marriageable young men from far and near. They were all lined up in the order of their rank: first came the kings, then the dukes, princes, counts, and barons, and last of all the knights. The king's daughter was led down the line, but to each suitor she had some objection. One was too fat and she called him a "wine barrel." The next was too tall: "Tall and skinny, that's a ninny." The third was short: "Short and thick won't do the trick." The fourth was too pale: "As pale as death." The fifth too red: "A turkey cock." The sixth wasn't straight enough: "Green wood, dried behind the stove." She found some fault with every one of them, but she made the most fun of a kindly king who was standing at the head of the line, and whose chin was slightly crooked. "Heavens above!" she cried. "He's got a chin like a thrush's bill!" And from then on he was known as "Thrushbeard."

When the old king saw that his daughter did nothing but make fun of people and rejected all the suitors who had come to the feast, he flew into a rage and swore to make her marry the first beggar who came to his door. A few days later a wandering minstrel came and sang under the window in the hope of earning a few coins. When the king heard him, he said: "Send him up." The minstrel appeared in his ragged, dirty clothes, sang for the king and his daughter, and asked for a gift when he had finished. The king said: "Your singing has pleased me so well that I'll give you my daughter for your wife." The princess was horrified, but the king said: "I swore I'd give you to the first beggar who came by, and I'm going to abide by my oath." All her pleading was in vain, the priest was called, and she was married to the minstrel then and there. After the ceremony the king said: "Now that you're a beggar woman, I can't have you living in my palace. You can just go away with your husband."

The beggar took her by the hand and led her out of the palace, and she had to go with him on foot. They came to a large forest, and she asked:

> "*Who does that lovely forest belong to?*"
> "*That forest belongs to King Thrushbeard.*
> *If you'd taken him, you could call it your own.*"
> "*Alas, poor me, if I'd only known,*
> *If only I'd taken King Thrushbeard!*"

Next they came to a meadow, and she asked:

> "*Who does that lovely green meadow belong to?*"
> "*That meadow belongs to King Thrushbeard.*
> *If you'd taken him, you could call it your own.*"
> "*Alas, poor me, if I'd only known,*
> *If only I'd taken King Thrushbeard!*"

She was married to the minstrel then and there.

Then they passed through a big city, and she asked:

> *"Who does this beautiful city belong to?"*
> *"This city belongs to King Thrushbeard.*
> *If you'd taken him, you could call it your own."*
> *"Alas, poor me, if only I'd known,*
> *If only I'd taken King Thrushbeard!"*

"You give me a pain," said the minstrel, "always wishing for another husband. I suppose I'm not good enough for you!" At last they came to a tiny little house, and she said:

> *"Good God, this shack is a disgrace!*
> *Who could own such a wretched place?"*

The minstrel answered: "It's my house and yours, where we shall live together." The king's daughter had to bend down to get through the low doorway. "Where are the servants?" she asked. "Servants, my foot!" answered the beggar. "If you want something done, you'll have to do it for yourself. And now make a fire and put on water for my supper because I'm dead tired." But the king's daughter didn't know the first thing about fires or cooking, and the beggar had to help her or he wouldn't have had any supper at all. When they had eaten what little there was, they went to bed. But bright and early the next morning he made her get up and clean the house. They worried along for a few days, but then their provisions were gone, and the man said: "Wife, we can't go on like this, eating and drinking and earning nothing. You'll have to weave baskets." He went out and cut willow withes and brought them home. She began to weave but the hard withes bruised her tender hands. "I see that won't do," said the man. "Try spinning, maybe you'll be better at it." She sat down and tried to spin, but the hard thread soon cut her soft fingers and drew blood. "Well, well!" said the man. "You're no good for any work. I've made a bad bargain. But now I think I'll buy up some earthenware pots and dishes. All you'll have to do is sit in the marketplace and sell them." "Goodness gracious!" she thought, "if somebody from my father's kingdom goes to the marketplace and sees me sitting there selling pots, how they'll laugh at me!" But there was no help for it, she had to give in or they would have starved.

The first day all went well; people were glad to buy her wares because she was beautiful; they paid whatever she asked, and some didn't even trouble to take the pots they had paid for. The two of them lived on the proceeds as long as the stock held out, and then the husband bought up a fresh supply of crockery. She took a place at the edge of the market, set out her wares around her and offered them for sale. All of a sudden a drunken hussar came galloping through, upset her pots and smashed them all into a thousand pieces. She began to cry, she was worried sick. "Oh!" she wailed, "what will become of me? What will my husband say!" She ran home and told him what had happened. "What did you expect?" he said. "Setting out earthenware pots at the edge of the market! But stop crying. I can see you're no good for any sensible work. Today I was at our king's palace. I asked if they could use a kitchen maid, and they said they'd take you. They'll give you your meals."

So the king's daughter became a kitchen maid and had to help the cook and do the most disagreeable work. She carried little jars in both her pockets to take home the leftovers they gave her, and that's what she and her husband lived on. It so happened that the marriage of the king's eldest son was about to be celebrated. The poor woman went upstairs and stood in the doorway of the great hall, looking on. When the candles were lit and the courtiers began coming in, each more magnificent than the last and everything was so bright and full of splendor, she was sad at heart. She thought of her miserable life and cursed the pride and arrogance that had brought her so low and made her so poor. Succulent dishes were being carried in and out and the smell drifted over to her. Now and then a servant tossed her a few scraps, and she put them into her little jars to take home. And then the king's son appeared; he was dressed in silk and velvet and had gold chains round his neck. When he saw the beautiful woman in the doorway, he took her by the hand and asked her to dance with him, but she refused. She was terrified, for she saw it was King Thrushbeard, who had courted her and whom she had laughed at and rejected. She tried to resist, but he drew her into the hall. Then the string that kept her pockets in place snapped, the jars fell to the floor, the soup spilled and the scraps came tumbling out. The courtiers all began to laugh and jeer, and she would sooner have been a hundred fathoms under the earth.

She bounded through the door and tried to escape, but on the stairs a man caught her and brought her back, and when she looked at him she saw it was King Thrushbeard again. He spoke kindly to her and said: "Don't be afraid. I am the minstrel you've been living with in that wretched shack; I disguised myself for love of you, and I was also the hussar who rode in and smashed your crockery. I did all that to humble your pride and punish you for the insolent way you laughed at me." Then she wept bitterly and said: "I've been very wicked and I'm not worthy to be your wife." But he said: "Don't cry, the hard days are over; now we shall celebrate our wedding." The maids came and dressed her magnificently, her father arrived with his whole court and congratulated her on her marriage to King Thrushbeard, and it was then that the feast became really joyful. I wish you and I had been there.

The Three Spinners

Once there was a lazy girl who didn't want to spin, and nothing her mother could say did a bit of good. In the end the mother became so angry and impatient that she beat her, and the daughter began to cry. The queen happened to be riding past. When she heard the girl's cries, she stopped her carriage, went into the house, and asked the mother why she was beating her daughter so hard that her screams could be heard out on the road. The woman was ashamed to say that her daughter was lazy, so she said: "I can't make her stop spinning; all she wants to do is spin and spin, but I'm poor and I can't afford all that flax."

The queen replied: "There's nothing I like more than the sound of spinning, and I'm never happier than when I hear the wheels whir. Let me take your daughter home with me to my palace. I've got plenty of flax, and I'll let her spin to her heart's content." The mother was delighted, and the queen took the girl away with her. When they got to the palace, she took her upstairs and showed her three rooms that were full of the finest flax, from floor to ceiling. "Just spin this flax," she said. "If you succeed, you shall have my eldest son for a husband. You may be poor, but what does it matter? You're a good hard worker, and that's all the dowry you need." The girl was frightened to death, for she couldn't have spun all that flax if she lived to be three hundred and sat there from morning to night. When she was left alone, she began to cry and she cried for three days without lifting a finger. On the third day the queen came in. She was surprised to see that none of the flax had been spun, but the girl explained that she hadn't been able to begin because leaving her mother had made her too sad. The queen accepted her excuse, but said as she was leaving: "I expect you to start working tomorrow."

When the girl was alone again, she didn't know what to do. In her distress she stood at the window, looking out, and she saw three women coming down the road. The first had a broad, flat foot; the second had a lower lip so big that it hung down over her chin; and the third had a broad thumb. They stopped outside the window, looked up, and asked her what the matter was. She told them about the trouble she was in, and they offered to help her. "We'll spin all your flax for you, and quickly too," they said, "if only you'll invite us to your wedding and not be ashamed of us and introduce us as your cousins and let us sit at your table." "With all my heart," she said. "Come in. You can start work right away."

So she let the three queer women in, and made a space in the first room for them to sit in and start spinning. The first drew the thread and plied the treadle, the second moistened the thread, the third twisted it and struck the table with her finger, and each time she struck the table a skein of yarn fell to the floor, and it was spun ever so finely. The girl hid the three spinners from the queen and showed her such a quantity of spun yarn every time she came in that she couldn't praise her enough. When the first room was empty, they started on the second, and then on the third, and it too was soon emptied. Then the three women took their leave and said to the girl: "Don't forget your promise. It will be your good fortune."

"We'll spin all your flax for you, and quickly too."

When the queen saw the empty rooms and the enormous pile of yarn, she arranged for the wedding. The bridegroom was glad to be getting such a clever hard-working wife and praised her mightily. "I have three cousins," the girl said. "They've been very good to me, and it wouldn't be right to forget them now, in my happiness. Would you let me invite them to the wedding and ask them to sit at my table?" The queen and the bridegroom said: "Why on earth wouldn't we let you?" When the festivities began, the three old maids appeared in outlandish costumes, and the bride said: "Welcome, dear cousins." "Good Lord!" said the bridegroom. "How did you ever come by such ungainly looking cousins?" He went over to the one with the broad, flat foot, and asked: "How did you get such a broad foot?" "By treading," she replied. "By treading." The bridegroom went over to the second and asked: "How did you ever get that hanging lip?" "By licking," she replied. "By licking." And he asked the third: "How did you get that broad thumb?" "By twisting thread," she replied. "By twisting thread." The prince was horrified. "In that case," he said, "my beautiful bride shall never touch a spinning wheel again." From then on there was no further question of her having to spin that horrid flax.

The Three Little Men
in the Woods

There was once a man whose wife died and a woman whose husband died, and the man had a daughter and the woman also had a daughter. The girls knew each other and went for a walk together and then they went to the woman's house. And the woman said to the man's daughter: "Listen to me. Go and tell your father I want to marry him. Then you will wash in milk every morning and drink wine, but my daughter will wash in water and drink water." The girl went home and told her father what the woman had said. The man said: "What should I do? Marriage is a joy, but it's also torture." Finally, when he couldn't make up his mind, he took off his boot and said: "See this boot? There's a hole in it. Take it up to the attic, hang it on a nail, and pour water into it. If the water stays, I'll take a wife; if it runs out, I won't." The girl did as she was bidden. The water pulled the sides of the hole together and the boot stayed brimful. She told her father what had happened. Then he went up to the attic to see for himself, and when he saw it was true, he went to the widow and courted her, and the wedding was celebrated.

Next morning, when the two girls got up, the husband's daughter had milk to wash in and wine to drink, and the wife's daughter had water to wash in and water to drink. On the second morning, the husband's daughter as well as the wife's daughter had water to wash in and water to drink. On the third morning, the husband's daughter had water to wash in and water to drink, and the wife's daughter had milk to wash in and wine to drink. And that's how it was from then on. The wife hated her stepdaughter like poison and racked her brains looking for ways to make things worse for her from day to day. For one thing, she was envious, because her stepdaughter was beautiful and sweet-tempered, while her own daughter was ugly and horrid.

One winter day, when the ground was frozen solid and hill and dale were covered with snow, the wife made a dress out of paper, called the girl and said: "Put on this dress and go out into the woods. I want you to bring me a little basket full of strawberries. I have a craving for them." "My goodness!" said the girl. "Strawberries don't grow in the wintertime; the ground is frozen and everything is covered with snow. And why do you want me to go out in this paper dress?—it's so cold your breath freezes. The wind will blow through it and the brambles will tear it off me." "Don't you dare talk back to me!" cried the stepmother. "Get a move on and don't show your face again until that basket is full of strawberries." Then she gave her a piece of stale bread. "This will do you for the day," she said. And she thought: "She'll die of cold and hunger out there, and I'll never see her again."

Obediently the stepdaughter put on the paper dress and went out with the little basket. As far as the eye could see, there was nothing but snow, and not the slightest blade of green. When she got to the woods, she saw a hut. Three dwarfs were peering out of it. She bade them good morning and knocked shyly at the door. "Come in!" they cried. She went in and sat down on the bench by the stove to warm herself and eat her breakfast. The dwarfs said: "Give us

Ripe strawberries, every one of them dark red,
coming up from under the snow.

some." "Gladly," she said, and broke her piece of bread in two and gave them half. "What are you doing out here in the woods in that thin dress in the dead of winter?" they asked. "I've been sent to look for strawberries," she said. "And I'm not to go home until I've picked a basketful." When she had eaten her bread, they gave her a broom and said: "Sweep the snow away from the back door." While she was outside, the three little men talked it over: "What should we give her for being so good and kind and sharing her bread with us?" The first said: "My gift is that she shall become more beautiful every day." The second said: "My gift is that whenever she says a word a gold piece shall fall out of her mouth." The third said: "My gift is that a king shall come and take her for his wife."

The girl did as the dwarfs had bidden her. She took the broom and swept the snow from behind the hut, and what do you think she found? Ripe strawberries, every one of them dark red, coming up from under the snow. In her joy she picked until her basket was full, thanked the little men, gave each of them her hand, and ran home to bring her stepmother what she had asked for. When she went in and said, "Good evening," a gold piece fell from her mouth. Then she told them what had happened in the woods, and as she spoke the gold pieces kept falling out of her mouth, so that the floor was soon covered with them. "Of all the arrogance!" said her stepsister. "Throwing money around like that!" But in her heart she envied her, and wanted to go out into the woods and look for strawberries. Her mother said: "No, no, my darling daughter, it's too cold, you'd freeze to death." But the daughter gave her no peace, and in the end she let her go. She made her a beautiful fur coat to wear, and gave her sandwiches and cake to take with her.

The girl went to the woods and headed straight for the hut. Again the three dwarfs were peering out, but she didn't say good morning or honor them with so much as a glance. Without a word of greeting she stomped into the hut, sat down by the stove, and began to eat her sandwiches and cake. "Give us some!" the little men cried out, but she replied: "How can I when I haven't enough for myself?" When she had finished eating, they said: "Here's a broom, go and sweep around the back door." "Pooh! Go do your own sweeping," she said. "I'm not your maid." When she saw they weren't going to give her anything, she went outside. The little men talked it over. "What shall we give her for being so horrid and having a wicked, envious heart, and never giving anything away?" The first said: "My gift is that she shall become uglier every day." The second said: "My gift is that whenever she says a word a toad shall jump out of her mouth." The third said: "My gift is that she shall die a cruel death." The girl looked for strawberries outside the hut, and when she didn't find any she went peevishly home. And when she opened her mouth to tell her mother what had happened, a toad jumped out at every word, and everyone thought she was disgusting.

The stepmother was angrier than ever. All she could think of was how to bring sorrow to her husband's daughter, who was growing more beautiful every day. In the end, she took a kettle, put it on the fire, and boiled yarn in it. When the yarn was boiled, she threw it over the poor girl's shoulder, gave her an ax, and told her to go out to the frozen river, cut a hole in the ice and rinse the yarn. Obediently she went to the river and began to chop a hole in the ice. While she was chopping, a marvelous carriage came along and a king was sitting in it. The carriage stopped and the king asked: "Who are you, my child, and what are you doing here?" "I'm a poor girl and I'm rinsing yarn." The king felt sorry for her, and when he saw how beautiful she was, he said: "Would you like to ride away with me?" "Oh yes, with all my heart," she said, for she was glad to get away from her mother and sister.

So she got into the carriage and rode away with the king, and when they got to his palace their wedding was celebrated with great splendor, and that was the little men's gift to the girl. A year later the young queen gave birth to a son, and when her stepmother heard of her great good fortune, she and her daughter came to the palace as if to pay her a visit. Then one day when the king had gone out and no one else was there, the wicked woman grabbed the queen by the head and her daughter grabbed her by the feet, and they picked her up from her bed and threw her out of the window into the river. Then the ugly daughter lay down in the bed, and the old woman pulled the blankets up over her head. When the king came home and wanted to speak to his wife, the old woman cried: "Hush, hush, not now. She's all in a sweat, you must let her rest." The king thought no harm and didn't come back until the next morning. Then he spoke to his wife and she answered, and at every word a toad jumped out of her mouth, when up until then it had always been a gold piece. He asked what was wrong with her, but the old woman said it came of the bad sweat she'd been in, and the trouble would soon go away.

That night the kitchen boy saw a duck swimming in the drainage runnel, and the duck said:

> "*What are you doing, king?*
> *Are you awake, or slumbering?*"

When he didn't answer, the duck said:

> "*What are my guests about?*"

And the kitchen boy answered:

> "*They're sound asleep, no doubt.*"

Then the duck asked:

"And what of my baby sweet?"

And he answered:

"He's in his cradle asleep."

Then the duck took the form of the queen and went up and suckled the child and plumped up his bed and covered him up. Then she turned into a duck again and swam away in the runnel. Next night she did the same thing, and on the third she said to the kitchen boy: "Go and tell the king to take his sword and stand on the threshold and swing it over me three times." The kitchen boy ran to the king and told him, and he came with his sword and swung it three times over the ghost. The third time his wife stood before him alive and well and as lovely as ever.

The king was very happy, but he kept the queen hidden in a bed-chamber until the Sunday when the child was to be christened. After the christening, the king said: "What should be done to a person who drags someone out of bed and throws him into the water?" The old woman answered: "The villain should be shut up in a barrel studded with nails and rolled down the hill into the water." The king said: "You've pronounced your own sentence." He sent for just such a barrel, and the old woman and her daughter were put into it, and the lid was hammered tight, and it was rolled down the hill into the river.

Clever Gretel

There was once a cook by the name of Gretel, who wore shoes with red heels, and when she went out in them she wiggled and waggled happily, and said to herself: "My, what a pretty girl I am." And when she got home again, she'd be in such a good humor that she'd take a drink of wine, and then, as wine whets the appetite, she'd taste all the best parts of what she was cooking until she was full, and say: "A cook has to know how her cooking tastes."

One day her master said to her: "Gretel, I'm having a guest for dinner. I want you to make us two nice roast chickens." "Yes, master, I'll be glad to," said Gretel. She slit the chickens' throats, scalded, plucked, and spitted them, and toward evening put them over the fire to roast. The chickens began to brown and were almost done, but the guest hadn't arrived. Gretel called in to her master: "If your guest doesn't come soon, I'll have to take the chickens off the fire, but it would be a crying shame not to eat them now, while they're at their juiciest best." "In that case," said the master, "I'll go and get him myself." The moment his back was turned, she put the spit with the chickens on it to one side. "Standing over the fire so long makes a body sweat," she thought, "and sweating makes a body thirsty. How do I know when they'll get here? In the meantime I'll hop down to the cellar and have a little drink." Down she ran, filled a jug from the barrel, said: "God bless it to your use, Gretel," and took a healthy swig. "Wine goes with wine," she said, "and never should they part," and took a healthier swig. Then she went upstairs, put the chickens back on the fire, brushed them with butter, and gave the spit a few lively turns. But the chickens smelled so good that she thought: "Maybe they're not seasoned quite right, I'd better taste them." She touched her fingers to one, licked them, and cried out: "Oh, how delicious these chickens are! It's a crying shame not to eat them this minute!"

She went to the window to see if the master and his guest were coming, but there was no one in sight. She went back to the chickens and thought: "That wing is burning. There's only one way to stop it." So she cut the wing off and ate it. It hit the spot, and when she had finished she thought: "I'll have to take the other one off too, or the master will see that something's missing." After doing away with the two wings, she went back to the window to look for her master. No master in sight, so then she had an idea. "How do I know? Maybe they're not coming. Maybe they've stopped at a tavern." She gave herself a poke: "Come on, Gretel. Don't be a spoilsport. One has been cut into; have another drink and finish it up. Once it's gone, you won't have anything to worry about. Why waste God's blessings?" Again she hopped down to the cellar, took a good stiff drink, and polished off the one chicken with joy in her heart. When one chicken was gone and there was still no sign of the master, Gretel looked at the other and said: "Where the one is, there the other should be. Chickens go in pairs, and what's good enough for one is good enough for the other. And besides, another drink won't hurt me any." Where-

---

The guest heard the master whetting his knife and ran down the steps as fast as his legs could carry him.

upon she took an enormous drink and started the second chicken on its way to rejoin the first.

She was still eating lustily when her master came along and called out: "Quick, Gretel. Our guest will be here in a minute." "Oh, yes, sir," said Gretel. "I'll serve you in a jiffy." The master looked in to make sure the table was properly set, took his big carving knife, and began to sharpen it in the pantry. The guest was a well-bred man. When he got to the house, he knocked softly. Gretel hurried to the door and looked out. When she saw the guest, she put her finger to her lips and said: "Sh-sh! Quick, go away! If my master catches you, you're done for. Do you know why he invited you to dinner? Because he wants to cut your ears off. Listen! That's him sharpening his knife!" The guest heard the master whetting his knife and ran down the steps as fast as his legs could carry him.

But Gretel wasn't through yet. She ran screaming to her master: "A fine guest you brought into the house!" she cried. "Why, what's the matter, Gretel? What do you mean?" "I mean," she said, "that just as I was getting ready to serve up the chickens he grabbed them and ran away with them." "That's a fine way to behave," said the master, grieved at the loss of his fine chickens. "If he'd only left me one of them! Then at least I'd have something to eat." "Stop! Stop!" he shouted, but the guest pretended not to hear. So still holding his knife the master ran after him, crying out: "Just one! Just one!" meaning that the guest should leave him one chicken and not take both. But the guest thought the master had decided to content himself with one ear, and seeing that he wanted to take both his ears home with him, he ran as if someone had made a fire under his feet.

One-eye, Two-eyes, and Three-eyes

There was once a woman who had three daughters, the eldest of whom was called One-eye, because she had only a single eye in the middle of her forehead, the second Two-eyes, because she had two eyes like other girls, and the youngest Three-eyes, because she had three eyes, two on the sides and the third in the middle of her forehead. As Two-eyes looked no different from other people, her sisters and her mother hated her. They said to her: "You with your two eyes are no better than the common herd. You're not one of us." They pushed her around, gave her raggedy old hand-me-downs to wear and nothing but their leavings to eat, and did everything they could to make her miserable.

One day Two-eyes was sent out to the meadow to look after the goat, though her sisters hadn't given her enough to eat and she was still very hungry. She sat down on a tuft of grass and began to cry, and she cried so hard that two little rivulets ran down her cheeks. When she looked up in her misery, a woman was standing there. "Why are you crying, Two-eyes?" she asked. "How can I help it?" said Two-eyes. "My mother and my two sisters hate me because I have two eyes like other people. They make me stand in the corner, they give me raggedy old hand-me-downs to wear and nothing but their leavings to eat. They gave me so little today that I'm still starving." The Wise Woman said: "Two-eyes, wipe your tears. I'm going to tell you something that will stop you from ever being hungry again. All you have to do is say these words to your goat:

> '*Little goat, bleat,*
> *Bring me a table*
> *With good things to eat,*'

and a neatly set table will appear with the finest food on it and you'll be able to eat as much as you like. Then when you've had enough and you don't need the table anymore, just say:

> '*Little goat, bleat,*
> *Take the table away,*
> *I've had all I can eat,*'

and the table will vanish." With that, the Wise Woman left her, and Two-eyes thought: "I'll try it out this minute and see if she was telling the truth, for I'm so dreadfully hungry." So she said:

> "*Little goat, bleat,*
> *Bring me a table*
> *With good things to eat.*"

And no sooner had she spoken than a table laid with a white table-

Three-eyes closed her third eye as if it too were asleep,
but that was only a trick.

cloth was standing there, and on it there was a plate, with a knife and a fork and a silver spoon, and the finest dishes were set on it, all hot and steaming, as if they had just come from the kitchen. Two-eyes said the shortest prayer she knew: "Dear God, be with us always. Amen," and fell to. She enjoyed every mouthful, and when she had had enough, she said the words the Wise Woman had taught her:

> *"Little goat, bleat,*
> *Take the table away,*
> *I've had all I can eat."*

The table and everything on it vanished instantly. Two-eyes was very happy. "My," she said, "what a lovely table!"

That evening when she got home with her goat, she found some food in an earthenware bowl that her sisters had set out for her, but she didn't touch it. The next day she went out again with her goat and didn't touch the few crumbs her sisters gave her. The first time and the second time they paid no attention, but when the same thing happened every day they couldn't help noticing. "There's something strange going on," they said. "Two-eyes always used to eat up everything we gave her, and now she leaves her food untouched. She must have found some other way." Bent on discovering the truth, they decided that when Two-eyes took the goat to pasture One-eye should go along and watch to see what she did and whether anyone brought her food and drink.

As Two-eyes was starting out, One-eye stepped up to her and said: "I think I'll go out to the meadow with you to make sure the goat is well grazed and properly taken care of." But Two-eyes knew what One-eye had in mind. She drove the goat into the tall grass and said: "Come, One-eye, let's sit down and I'll sing you a song." One-eye sat down. The unaccustomed walk and the heat of the sun had made her tired, and Two-eyes sang over and over again:

"One-eye, are you awake?
One-eye, are you asleep?"

One-eye closed her one eye and fell asleep. When Two-eyes saw that One-eye was asleep and couldn't spy on her, she said:

"Little goat, bleat,
  Bring me a table
  With good things to eat,"

and sat down at her table, and ate and drank till she had enough, and then she cried out:

"Little goat, bleat,
  Take the table away,
  I've had all I can eat,"

and in an instant everything had vanished. Then Two-eyes woke One-eye, and said: "One-eye, you were going to take care of the goat, and look how you do it. You fall asleep. Why, the goat could have run God knows where. Come, let's go home." And home they went. Again Two-eyes left her bowl untouched, but One-eye couldn't tell her mother why she didn't eat, and the only excuse she could make for herself was: "I fell asleep out there."

The next day the mother said to Three-eyes: "This time I want you to go and see if Two-eyes eats anything out there and if someone brings her food and drink, because she must be eating and drinking in secret." So Three-eyes went over to Two-eyes and said: "I think I'll go with you to make sure the goat is well grazed and properly taken care of." But Two-eyes knew what Three-eyes had in mind. She drove the goat into the tall grass and said: "Come, Three-eyes, let's go and sit down. I'll sing you a song." Three-eyes sat down. The walk and the heat of the sun had made her tired, and Two-eyes began to sing the same song as before:

> *"Three-eyes, are you awake?"*

But instead of singing:

> *"Three-eyes, are you asleep?"*

as she should have, she was careless and sang:

> *"Two-eyes, are you asleep?"*

So that what she kept singing was:

> *"Three-eyes, are you awake?*
> *Two-eyes, are you asleep?"*

So two of Three-eyes' eyes closed and fell asleep, but the third didn't, because it wasn't mentioned in the song. Three-eyes closed her third eye as if it too were asleep, but that was only a trick, and it blinked and saw everything that went on.

When Two-eyes thought Three-eyes was sound asleep, she said her little rhyme:

> *"Little goat, bleat.*
> *Bring me a table*
> *With good things to eat."*

And when she had eaten and drunk to her heart's content, she sent the table away again, saying:

> *"Little goat, bleat,*
> *Take the table away,*
> *I've had all I can eat."*

And Three-eyes had seen it all. Then Two-eyes went and woke her up and said: "Goodness, Three-eyes, have you been asleep? Is that how you take care of the goat? Come, let's go home." Home they went, and again Two-eyes ate nothing, and Three-eyes said to her mother: "Now I know why the haughty thing doesn't eat. She says to the goat:

> *'Little goat, bleat,*
> *Bring me a table*
> *With good things to eat,'*

and before you know it a table is standing there spread with the finest food, much better than we have here, and when she's had enough, she says:

> *'Little goat, bleat,*
> *Take the table away,*
> *I've had all I can eat,'*

and then everything disappears. I saw it all. She put two of my eyes asleep with magic words, but luckily the one in the middle of my forehead stayed awake." At that the envious mother cried out: "What's this! You think you can have it better than we do? Well, you won't think so much longer." And she took the butcher knife and thrust it into the goat's heart, and it fell dead.

Two-eyes was overcome with grief. She went out to the meadow, sat down on her tuft of grass and wept bitter tears. Suddenly the

Wise Woman was standing beside her. "Why are you crying, Two-eyes?" she asked. "Haven't I reason to cry?" she replied. "My mother has slaughtered the goat that brought me such nice things to eat, and now I'll be hungry and miserable again." The Wise Woman said: "Two-eyes, I will give you a piece of good advice. Get your sisters to give you the dead goat's entrails, then bury them outside the front door. They will bring you good fortune." Then she vanished. Two-eyes went home and said to her sisters: "Dear sisters, would you give me some of my goat? I won't ask you for any of the good parts. Just let me have the entrails." They laughed and said: "If the entrails are all you want, take them." Two-eyes took the entrails and that evening she quietly buried them outside the front door, just as the Wise Woman had advised her.

Next morning when they all woke up and went outside, a marvelous tree was growing there. It had silver leaves and golden fruit, and nothing in all the world could have been more splendid or more beautiful. They couldn't imagine how the tree had got there during the night. Only Two-eyes knew it had grown from the goat's entrails, because it was growing in the exact place where she had buried them. "Climb up, child," said the mother to One-eye, "and pick us some of the fruit." One-eye climbed the tree, but when she tried to pick a golden apple, the branch slipped out of her grasp. Time and time again the same thing happened, and try as she might she couldn't manage to pick a single apple. "Three-eyes," said the mother, "you climb up. You with your three eyes are sure to be more keen-sighted than your sister." One-eye slid down and Three-eyes climbed the tree. But she was no more nimble, and for all her keen sight, the golden apples escaped her. Finally the mother lost patience and climbed the tree herself, but she was no more able to grasp the fruit than One-eye and Three-eyes, and her hands kept clutching at the air. After a while Two-eyes spoke up: "Suppose I try. Maybe I'll have better luck." The sisters cried out: "You with your two eyes! How perfectly silly!" Nevertheless, Two-eyes climbed the tree, and far from recoiling from her, the golden apples met her hand halfway. She was able to pick as many as she pleased and when she climbed down her apron was full of them. Her mother took them, but instead of treating her better she and One-eye and Three-eyes were made so envious by Two-eyes' success in picking the fruit, that they dealt with her more harshly than ever.

It so happened that one day as they were standing at the foot of the tree, a young knight came by. "Two-eyes!" cried the sisters. "Hide or you'll disgrace us." Quick as a flash they picked up an empty barrel that happened to be standing near the tree and threw it over her, and they shoved the golden apples she had just picked under it too. When the knight came closer, he proved to be very handsome. He stopped to admire the splendid gold and silver tree and said to the two sisters: "Whom does this beautiful tree belong to? If anyone were to give me a branch from it, I'd give that person anything they wished in return." One-eye and Three-eyes said the tree belonged to them and undertook to break off a branch for him. They tried and tried, but in vain, for the branches and fruit shrank back from them every time they approached. At that the knight said: "If the tree belongs to you, it seems strange that you can't break off a part of it." They said again that the tree was theirs. But as they were speaking, Two-eyes, who was angry at One-eye and Three-eyes for not telling the truth, pushed a few of the golden apples out from under the barrel, and they rolled to the knight's feet.

He was astonished at the sight and asked where they came from. One-eye and Three-eyes replied that there was another sister, who wasn't allowed to show herself because she had two eyes like ordinary people. But the knight insisted on seeing her and cried: "Two-eyes, come out!" Confidently, Two-eyes came out from under the barrel. The knight was amazed at her great beauty and said: "You, Two-eyes,

I'm sure, can break off a branch of the tree for me." "Yes," said Two-eyes, "I believe I can, because it's my tree." She climbed up and had no trouble at all in breaking off a branch covered with fine silver leaves and golden fruit. She handed it to the knight, and he said: "What shall I give you for it, Two-eyes?" "Dear me," said Two-eyes, "I've been suffering hunger and thirst, misery and privation from early morning to late at night. If you take me away with you and save me from all that, I shall be very happy." The knight lifted her up on his saddle and carried her off to his father's castle, where he gave her fine clothes and food and drink to her heart's content. He loved her so much that he married her, and the wedding was celebrated with great rejoicing.

When the handsome knight rode away with Two-eyes, the sisters envied her in bitter earnest. "But at least," they thought, "we still have the wonderful tree. Even if we can't pick the fruit, everyone will stop to look at it, and come in to see us, and sing its praises. Who knows what good fortune may lie in wait for us?" But next morning the tree had vanished and their hopes were dashed. And when Two-eyes looked out of her window, there to her great joy was the tree, for it had followed her.

Two-eyes lived happily for many years. One day two poor women came to the castle, begging for alms. Two-eyes looked into their faces and recognized her sisters One-eye and Three-eyes, who had become so poor they were obliged to wander from door to door, begging their daily bread. Two-eyes welcomed them and treated them kindly and cared for them, and with all their hearts they regretted the evil they had done their sister in their youth.

The Six Swans

A king once went hunting in a large forest and pursued a stag so furiously that none of his men could keep up with him. Toward nightfall, he stopped and looked around, and saw that he was lost. He searched for a way out of the forest but found none. Then he saw an old woman and her head wagged from side to side as she came toward him; she was a witch. "Good woman," he said to her, "can you show me the way out of this forest?" "Yes, indeed, Your Highness," she replied. "That I can, but on one condition, and if you don't meet it you'll never get out of the forest and you'll die of hunger." "What is the condition?" the king asked. "I have a daughter," said the old woman, "who is so beautiful you won't find her equal in the whole world. She is worthy to be your wife, and if you make her your queen I'll show you the way out of the forest." In fear and dread the king consented, and the old woman led him to her hut. Her daughter, who was sitting by the fire, welcomed the king as if she had been expecting him. He saw that she was indeed very beautiful, but he didn't like her and he couldn't look at her without a secret shudder. When he picked the girl up and put her in front of him on his horse, the old woman showed him the way. He returned to his royal palace and the wedding was celebrated.

The king had been married once before and had seven children by his first wife, six boys and a girl, whom he loved more than any-thing in the world. Fearing that their stepmother might mistreat or even harm them, he took them to a solitary castle deep in the forest. It was so well hidden and the way was so hard to find that he him-self couldn't have found it if a wise woman hadn't given him a ball of magic yarn. When he tossed the ball before him, the yarn un-wound itself and showed him the way. The king went out so often to see his beloved children that the queen noticed his absence. She was curious and wondered what he did out there in the forest all alone. She gave his servants a lot of money and they told her the se-cret. They also told her about the ball of yarn, which alone could show the way, and she had no peace until she had found out where the king kept it. Then she made little white silk shirts, and sewed a magic spell into them, for she had learned witchcraft from her mother.

One day when the king had gone hunting she took the little shirts and went out into the forest, and the ball of yarn showed her the way. When the children saw someone coming in the distance, they thought it was their father and ran happily to meet him. She threw a shirt over each of them, and the moment the shirts touched them they turned into swans and flew away over the trees. The queen went home delighted, thinking she was rid of her stepchildren, but the king's daughter hadn't run out with her brothers, and the queen didn't know she existed. Next day the king went to see his children, but he found only the girl. "Where are your brothers?" he asked. "Oh, Father dear," she said, "they've gone away and left me all alone." And she told him how she had stood at her window and seen her brothers turn into

---

A year later, when the queen brought her first child into the world, the old woman took it away.

swans and fly away over the trees, and she showed him the feathers which they had dropped in the courtyard and which she had picked up. The king grieved but he didn't think the queen had done this wicked thing and, fearing the girl would also be stolen from him, he decided to take her home with him. But she was afraid of her stepmother and asked him to let her spend one last night in the castle.

The poor girl thought to herself: "I can't stay here any longer; I must go and look for my brothers." When night came, she slipped away and went straight into the forest. She walked all night and the next day as well, until she was too tired to go on. Then she caught sight of a hut and when she opened the door she saw a room with six little beds in it. She didn't dare lie down on any of the beds, but crawled under one of them, stretched out on the hard ground and thought she'd spend the night there. But just before sundown she heard a flapping of wings and saw six swans come flying in the window. They settled on the ground and blew at each other and blew off all their feathers, and their swan skins came off like shirts. The girl looked at them and recognized her brothers. She was overjoyed to see them and crawled out from under the bed. The brothers were just as happy to see their little sister, but their joy was short-lived. "You can't stay here," they said. "This is a robbers' den. If they come home and find you, they'll murder you." "Can't you protect me?" she asked. "No," they said, "because we can only take our swan skins off for a quarter of an hour every evening, and then we're turned back into swans." The sister wept and said: "But can't you be set free?" "Oh no," they said. "There is a way, but it's too hard. You'd have to go without speaking or laughing for six years, and during that time you'd have to sew us six little shirts out of starflowers. If a single word crossed your lips, all your pains would be wasted." When the brothers had finished speaking, the quarter of an hour was over. They were turned back into swans and flew out of the window.

The girl decided to set her brothers free, even if it cost her her life. She left the hut, went out into the middle of the forest, climbed a tree and spent the night there. Next morning she climbed down, gathered starflowers and began to sew. There was no one to talk to and she was in no mood for laughing; she just sat there, attending to her work. One day, after she had been there a long time, the king of the country went hunting in the forest and his huntsmen came to the tree where she was sitting. They called out to her and said: "Who are you?" But she didn't answer. "Come down," they said. "We won't hurt you." But she only shook her head. When they kept pressing her with questions, she tossed down her gold necklace, thinking that would satisfy them. When they persisted, she threw down her girdle, and when that did no good her garters and little by little everything she was wearing, until she had nothing on but her shift. But the hunters refused to be put off; they climbed up, carried her down and took her to the king. The king asked her: "Who are you? What were you doing in that tree?" But she didn't answer. And though he asked her in all the languages he knew, she remained as silent as a fish. But she was so beautiful that the king's heart was moved, and he was filled with a great love for her. He threw his cloak over her, picked her up on his horse and carried her to his palace. There he had her dressed in rich garments and her beauty was as radiant as the day, but not a single word could be coaxed out of her. He seated her next to him at the table, and her gentle, demure ways were so much to his liking that he said: "This is the girl I want for my wife and none other in all the world," and a few days later they were married.

But the king had a wicked mother, who was displeased at this marriage and spoke ill of the young queen. "This slut who can't talk!" she said. "Who knows where she comes from? She's not worthy of a king." And a year later when the queen brought her first child into the world, the old woman took it away and daubed the queen's mouth with blood as she slept. Then she went to the king and accused the queen of eating her baby. The king refused to believe it and wouldn't let anyone harm her. As for the queen, she spent her days over her sewing and paid no attention to anything else. Her second child was a handsome boy and the wicked mother-in-law practiced the same deception, but the king couldn't bring himself to believe her. "She is much too good and pious to do such a thing," he said. "If she could speak and defend herself, her innocence would be plain." But when the old woman stole the newborn child for the third time and accused the queen and the queen didn't say a single word in self-defense, the king couldn't help himself. He had to let justice take its course, and the judges sentenced her to death by fire.

When the day came for the sentence to be carried out, it was also the last day of the six years during which she could neither speak nor laugh, and she had set her dear brothers free from the magic spell. The six shirts were finished, except for one that still lacked its left sleeve. When she was led to the stake, she carried the shirts over her arm. As she stood there and they were just coming to light the fire, she looked up and saw six swans come flying through the air. She knew she would soon be saved and her heart swelled for joy. The swans flew down and came so close that she was able to throw their shirts over them. The moment the shirts touched them their swan skins fell off, and there stood her brothers, strong and handsome. Only the youngest lacked his left arm and had a swan's wing in place of it. They hugged and kissed, and the queen went to the king, who was utterly bewildered. She opened her mouth and said: "Dearest husband, now I can speak and tell you that I am innocent and falsely accused." Then she told him about the old woman's deception, and how she had taken away her three children and hidden them. To the king's great joy the three children were produced and for her punishment the wicked mother-in-law was tied to the stake and burned to ashes. And the king and the queen and her six brothers lived for many years in peace and happiness.

"I'm making a trough for Father and Mother to eat out of when I'm big."

The Old Man
and His Grandson

There was once a very old man who was almost blind and deaf and whose knees trembled. When he sat at the table, he could hardly hold his spoon; he spilled soup on the tablecloth, and when he'd taken a spoonful some of it ran out of his mouth. His son and his son's wife thought it was disgusting and finally made the old man sit in a corner behind the stove. They brought him his food in an earthenware bowl and, worst of all, they didn't even give him enough. He looked sadly in the direction of the table, and his eyes filled with tears. One day his hands trembled so much that he dropped his bowl and it fell to the floor and broke. The young woman scolded him, but he said nothing and only sighed. She bought him a wooden bowl for a few kreuzers, and from then on he had to eat out of it. As they were sitting there one day, the little four-year-old grandson was on the floor playing with some pieces of wood. "What are you doing?" his father asked. The child replied: "I'm making a trough for Father and Mother to eat out of when I'm big." Husband and wife looked at each other for a while and burst into tears. After that they brought the old grandfather back to the table. He ate with them from then on, and even when he spilled a little something they said nothing.

The Nixie of the Pond

There was once a miller who lived happily with his wife. They had money and property, and their wealth increased from year to year. But misfortune comes overnight. Just as their wealth had increased, so it dwindled from year to year, and a time came when the miller could hardly call the mill where he lived his own. He was bowed with care and when he went to bed after the day's work, he tossed and turned and found no rest.

One morning he got up before daybreak and went out, hoping to find some relief out of doors. As he was crossing the mill dam, the first rays of sun appeared on the horizon. Just then he heard a sound in the pond, and turning around he saw a beautiful woman rise slowly from the water. With her delicate, well-shaped hands she was holding her long hair close to her shoulders, and it poured down over both sides of her pale white body. He saw it was the nixie of the pond, and he was so frightened he didn't know whether to stay or run. But the nixie spoke to him in a soft voice, called him by name, and asked him why he was so sad. At first the miller was struck dumb, but she sounded so friendly that he took heart and told her how he had once been rich but was now so poor he didn't know what to do. "Cheer up," said the nixie. "I'll make you richer than you ever were, but you must promise to give me what has just been born in your house." "What could that be but a puppy or a kitten?" thought the miller, and promised to give her what she had asked.

The nixie slipped back into the water, and he went home to his mill with a light heart. He was almost at the door when the serving maid came out and said: "Congratulations! Your wife has just given birth to a baby boy." The miller stood as though thunderstruck. He realized that the sly nixie had known it all along and had tricked him. Deep in gloom, he went to his wife's bedside, and when she said: "Isn't it a fine little boy? Why aren't you happy?" he told her about his meeting with the nixie and the promise he had made. "Riches will mean nothing to me," he said, "if I am to lose my child. But what can I do?" And the relatives who came to congratulate them had no suggestions to offer.

Prosperity returned to the miller's house. All his undertakings were successful, his chests and coffers seemed to fill themselves, and the money in his strongbox increased overnight. Soon he was richer than ever before. But he couldn't enjoy his wealth, for the promise he had given the nixie never ceased to torment him. Every time he passed the pond he was afraid she would appear to remind him of his debt. He never let the little boy go near the water. "Watch out," he said. "If you touch the water, a hand will come out and grab you and pull you under." But as year after year passed and the nixie didn't show herself, the miller began to feel easier in his mind.

The child grew to be a young man and was apprenticed to a hunter. When he had completed his apprenticeship and become an expert hunter, the lord of the village took him into his service. In the village there was a beautiful, truehearted girl, and the hunter

He saw a beautiful woman rise slowly from the water.

took a liking to her. When his master saw that, he gave him a small house and they were married. They loved each other with all their hearts and lived together in quiet happiness.

One day the hunter was chasing a deer. When the deer left the woods and came out into the open, he followed it and killed it with a single shot. He didn't notice that he was near the dangerous pond. After gutting the deer, he went to the water to wash his blood-stained hands, and he had scarcely dipped them in the water when the nixie rose up laughing, clasped him in her dripping arms, and pulled him down so quickly that the water rose up in waves.

When dusk fell and the hunter hadn't come home, his wife began to be worried and went looking for him. She half-suspected what had happened, for he had often told her about the nixie and how he kept away from the pond, and when she found his gamebag lying on the bank she could have no further doubt. Wailing and wringing her hands, she called her darling's name, but in vain. She ran to the other side of the water and called again; she shouted angry words at the nixie, but there was no answer. The surface of the water remained unruffled, and only the face of the half moon looked up at her.

The poor woman didn't leave the pond. She walked quickly round and round it, sometimes in silence, sometimes screaming, sometimes whimpering softly. Finally, when her strength gave out, she sank to the ground and fell into a deep sleep. Soon a dream came to her.

Stricken with fear, she was climbing a rocky mountain slope. Thornbushes and creepers clung to her feet, the rain beat down on her face, and the wind ruffled her long hair. When she reached the top, everything changed. The sky was blue, the air soft, the ground sloped gently downward, and in the midst of a green meadow strewn with bright-colored flowers she saw a clean little hut. She went and opened the door, and there sat a white-haired old crone, who gave her a friendly smile. At that moment the poor woman woke up. The day had already dawned, and she immediately decided to do what she had done in her dream. She had a hard time climbing the mountain, and everything was just as she had seen it in her dream. The old crone welcomed her kindly and showed her a chair to sit in. "Only some misfortune," she said, "can have brought you to my lonely hut." In tears the hunter's wife told her what had happened. "Dry your tears," said the old crone. "I will help you. Here you have a golden comb. Wait till the full moon rises. Then go to the pond, sit down at the edge, and comb your long black hair with this comb. When you have finished, lie down on the bank, and you'll see what happens."

The woman went home, but the days till the full moon were slow in passing. At last the glowing disk appeared in the sky. She went out to the pond, sat down, and combed her long black hair with the golden comb. When she had finished, she put the comb down at the edge of the water. Soon there was a gurgling from the depths, a wave arose, rolled to the bank, and carried the comb away. In no more time than the comb needed to sink to the bottom, the surface of the water parted and the hunter's head rose up. He didn't speak, but he gazed sadly at his wife. At that same moment a second wave came along and covered his head. He vanished, the pond lay as still as before, and there was nothing to be seen on its surface but the face of the full moon.

Sick at heart, the woman went home. But that night she saw the old crone's hut in her dream. Next morning she went to see her again, and poured out her heart. The old crone gave her a golden flute and said: "Wait until the full moon comes again. Then take this flute, sit down on the bank, and play a pretty tune on it. When you've finished, lie down on the sand. You'll see what happens."

She did as the old woman had told her. No sooner had she laid the flute on the sand than a gurgling was heard from the depths. A wave arose, rolled to the bank, and carried the flute away. A moment later the water parted and not only the head rose up, but with it half the man's body. Full of yearning, he opened his arms to her, but a second wave came rolling, covered him, and carried him down again.

"Ah," the poor woman sighed, "what good does it do me to glimpse my darling only to lose him again!" Again she was sick at heart, but for the third time her dream showed her the old crone's house. She went to her, and the wise woman gave her a golden spinning wheel, comforted her, and said: "The end is not yet. Wait till the full moon rises, then take this spinning wheel, sit down on the bank and spin until the spindle is full. When you have finished, leave the spinning wheel near the water, and you'll see what happens."

The woman did exactly as she had been told. As soon as the full moon appeared, she took the golden spinning wheel to the bank and spun without stopping until her flax was gone and the spindle was full of thread. No sooner had she set the spinning wheel down on the bank than a gurgling, more violent than before, was heard from the depths of the pond and a great wave came rolling and carried the spinning wheel away. A moment later the hunter's head and his whole body rose up in a waterspout. He jumped up on the bank, took his wife by the hand, and fled. But they had only gone a little way when the whole pond rose up with a terrible gushing and roaring, and overflowed the fields with irresistible force. The fugitives thought they would surely die, but in her terror the woman called on the old crone for help, and in that moment they were transformed, she into a toad, he into a frog. When the flood overtook them, it couldn't kill them, but it carried them far away and separated them.

When the waters subsided and they touched dry land again, their human forms came back to them. But neither knew where the other was and they were both among strange people who had never heard of their country. High mountains and deep valleys lay between them. For their livelihood both had to tend sheep. Full of grief and yearning, they drove their flocks through fields and forests for long years.

One day when spring had once more burst forth from the earth, they both went out with their flocks, and as luck would have it, they headed for the same place. Catching sight of a flock on a distant mountain slope, he headed for it with his sheep. They met in the valley below, but they didn't recognize each other. Nevertheless they were glad, for they weren't alone any longer. Every day from then on, they drove their flocks side by side. They didn't talk much, but they felt comforted. One night when the full moon was shining in the sky and the sheep had lain down to rest, the shepherd took the flute from his pocket and played a lovely but mournful tune. When he had finished, he saw the shepherdess was weeping bitterly. "Why are you weeping?" he asked. "Ah," she replied, "the full moon was shining just like this when I last played that tune on the flute and my darling's head rose out of the pond." He looked at her, and it seemed to him that a veil had fallen from his eyes. He recognized his dearest wife, and when she looked at his face in the moonlight, she also recognized him. They hugged and kissed each other, and there's no need to ask if they were happy.

Iron Hans

There was once a king who had a great forest near his palace. There was game of all kinds in the forest, and one day he sent a huntsman to shoot a roe, but the huntsman didn't come back. "Something must have happened to him," said the king, and the next day he sent two other huntsmen to look for him, but they didn't come back either. The third day he sent for all the rest of his huntsmen and said: "Search the whole forest, don't stop till you've found all three of them." But neither they nor any of the dogs they had taken with them were ever seen again. From that time on, everyone was afraid to go near the forest, which lay silent and forsaken, though now and then an eagle or a hawk could be seen flying over it. This went on for years, and then one day a strange huntsman appeared before the king, asking for employment and offering to go into the perilous forest. But the king wouldn't let him. "The place is haunted," he said. "I'm afraid you would fare no better than the others and would never come back." "Sire," said the huntsman, "I'll go at my own risk. I know nothing of fear."

The huntsman took his dog and went into the forest. The dog soon picked up a scent and started to follow it, but after running a few steps he came to a deep pool and had to stop. A bare arm rose from the water, grabbed hold of him and pulled him under. When the huntsman saw what had happened, he went back and brought three men with buckets, who emptied the water out of the pool. When they could see to the bottom, a wild man was lying there. His body was as brown as rusty iron, and his hair covered his face and hung down to his knees. They bound him with cords and carried him to the palace, where everyone was amazed at the sight of him, and the king had him shut up in an iron cage in the courtyard. All were forbidden on pain of death to open the door of the cage, and the key was entrusted to the queen herself. From that day on, it was safe to walk in the forest.

The king had an eight-year-old son who was playing in the court-yard one day, and as he was playing his golden ball fell into the cage. The little boy ran to the cage and said: "Give me my golden ball." "Not till you open the door for me," said the wild man. "No," said the boy, "I won't do that, the king has forbidden it." And he ran away. Next day he came again and asked for his ball. The wild man said: "Open my door," but the little boy wouldn't do it. On the third day the king was out hunting. The boy went back to the cage and said: "I couldn't open the door even if I wanted to, because I haven't got the key." "It's under your mother's pillow," said the wild man. "You can get it." The child, who desperately wanted his ball, threw caution to the winds, and went and got the key. He had trouble opening the door and caught his finger. When the door was open, the wild man came out, gave him the ball, and ran away. The child took fright and screamed and yelled: "Wild man, wild man, don't go away, they'll give me a whipping!" The wild man turned back, picked the child up, set him on his shoulders,

The wild man turned back, picked the child up, set him on his shoulders, and hurried away to the forest with long strides.

and hurried away to the forest with long strides. When the king came home, he saw the empty cage and asked the queen what had happened. She didn't know a thing, and when she looked for the key it was gone. She called the little boy, but no one answered. The king sent men to look for him in the fields, but they didn't find him. He had no trouble guessing what had happened, and the palace was filled with mourning.

When the wild man got back to the dark forest, he took the child down from his shoulders, put him on the ground, and said: "You'll never see your father and mother again, but I'll keep you with me because you set me free and I feel sorry for you. If you do exactly as I tell you, you'll be all right. I have plenty of gold and treasure, more than anyone in the world." He made the child a bed of moss to sleep on, and in the morning led him to a spring. "You see this golden spring?" he said. "It's as bright and clear as crystal. I want you to sit beside it and make sure nothing falls into it, for then the spring would be defiled. I'll come to you every evening to see if you've obeyed my order." The child sat down at the edge of the spring. Now and then he saw a golden fish or a golden snake in the water, and he was careful not to let anything fall in. Once, as he was sitting there, his finger hurt him so badly that without meaning to he dipped it in the water. Though he pulled it right out again, he saw the finger had turned to gold, and try as he might he couldn't wipe the gold off.

When Iron Hans came back that evening, he looked at the boy and said: "What has happened to the spring?" "Nothing. Nothing," he replied, holding his finger behind his back to keep Iron Hans from seeing it. But the wild man said: "You've dipped your finger in the water. I'll let it pass this once, but it mustn't happen again." Bright and early next morning he was sitting by the spring, keeping watch. His finger hurt him again, he ran it over his head, and as ill luck would have it, one of his hairs fell into the spring. He quickly pulled it out, but it was all gold. The moment Iron Hans got there he knew what had happened. "You've dropped a hair in the spring," he said. "I'll let it pass this once, but if it happens again the spring will be defiled, and you won't be able to stay with me any longer."

The third day the boy was sitting beside the spring, and much as his finger hurt him, he didn't move it. But the time hung heavy on his hands and he began to look at the reflection of his face in the water. He wanted to look himself straight in the eye and bent down farther and farther. All at once his long hair tumbled over his shoulders and fell into the water. Quickly he raised his head, but his hair had all been turned to gold and it glittered like the sun. You can imagine how terrified the poor boy was. He took his handkerchief and tied it around his head to keep the wild man from seeing it. But the moment the wild man got there he knew what had happened, and said: "Take off that handkerchief." The golden hair came flowing out, and nothing the boy could say was of any use. "You can't stay here any longer, for you haven't stood the test. Go out into the world. You'll find out what it is to be poor. But there's no wickedness in your heart and I wish you well, so I'll grant you one favor: if you're in trouble, come to the edge of the forest and shout: 'Iron Hans!' Then I'll come and help you. My power is great, greater than you think, and I have vast stores of gold and silver."

The prince left the forest and journeyed over beaten and unbeaten paths, until at last he came to a great city. There he looked for work but found none, for he had never learned anything that might have helped him earn his keep. In the end he went to the royal palace and asked for employment. The courtiers didn't know what to do with him, but they liked him and said he could stay. In the end the cook put him to work hauling wood and water and sweeping up the ashes. Once when no one else was available, the cook bade him carry the food platters to the royal table, and the boy kept his hat on because he didn't want anyone to see his golden hair. The king had never seen such behavior, and he said: "When you come to the royal table, you must take your hat off." "Oh, sire," he replied, "I can't do that. My head is covered with ugly scurf." The king summoned the cook and scolded him. "How could you ever take on a boy like that?" he cried. "Get rid of him immediately!" But the cook was sorry for the youngster and traded him for the gardener's boy.

Now he had to sow and plant, water the garden, and spade and hoe in good weather and bad. One summer day when he was working in the garden alone, the heat was so oppressive that he took off his hat to cool his head in the breeze. When the sunlight fell on his hair, it sparkled so bright that the glint reached the princess's bed-chamber and the princess jumped up to see what it was. She caught sight of the boy and cried out: "Boy, go and get me a bunch of flowers!" Quickly he put on his hat, picked a bunch of wildflowers and tied a string around them. On his way up the stairs he passed the gardener, who said: "How can you bring the princess such common flowers? Quick, get different ones! Choose the rarest and most beautiful." "Oh, no," said the boy. "Wildflowers are more fragrant, she'll like these better." When he went in, the princess said: "Take your hat off. It's not proper for you to keep it on in my presence." "I can't," he said. "I've got scurf all over my head." But she took hold of his hat and snatched it off. His golden hair tumbled down over his shoulders, a beautiful sight. He tried to run away, but she held him by the arm and gave him a handful of ducats. He took them, but he cared nothing for gold and gave them to the gardener, saying: "Here's a present for your children, something for them to play with." Next day the princess called to him again and asked him to get her a bunch of wildflowers. The moment he came in, she snatched at his hat and tried to take it off, but he held it fast with both hands. Again she gave him a handful of ducats, but he didn't want to keep them, so he gave them to the gardener for his children to play with. The third day the same thing happened. She couldn't take his hat off, and he wouldn't keep her gold.

A short while later, the land was overrun by war. The king mustered his troops, though he didn't know if they could stand up against the enemy, who was very powerful and had a large army. The gardener's boy said: "I'm grown up now, and I'm going to war. Just give me a horse." The others said: "Go and take one while we're away. We'll leave one in the stable for you." When they were gone, he went to the stable and took the horse. It was lame in one leg and limped, clippety-clop, clippety-clop, but he mounted all the same and rode away to the dark forest. When he got to the edge of it, he shouted three times: "Iron Hans!" so loudly that the sound went echoing through the trees. A moment later the wild man appeared, and said: "What do you want?" "I want a sturdy horse, for I'm riding off to war." "That you shall have and more," said the wild man. He went back into the forest, and in next to no time a groom appeared, leading a horse that was snorting and prancing and could hardly be held in check. Behind him came a squadron of iron-clad riders, and their swords flashed in the sunlight. The youth gave the groom his three-legged nag, mounted the charger, and rode off at the head of his troops.

When he reached the battlefield, a good part of the king's army had fallen, and those who remained would soon have had to give way. The youth and his iron squadron fell on the enemy like a whirlwind, striking down everyone in their path. The enemy turned and fled, but the youth pursued them and kept at it until not a man of them was left. Then, instead of returning to the king, he led his men over byways to the forest, and there he shouted for Iron Hans. "What do you want?" the wild man asked. "Take back your horse and your soldiers and give me my three-legged nag." All this was done, and he rode his three-legged nag back to the stable.

When the king returned to his palace, his daughter came to meet him and congratulated him on his victory. "The victory was none of my doing," said the king. "It was won by a strange knight who came to my help with his squadron." The daughter asked who the strange knight was, but the king didn't know. All he could say was: "He rode off in pursuit of the enemy and I never saw him again." She asked the gardener about his boy, but he laughed and said: "He's just come home on his three-legged nag. The others all made fun of him. 'Here's our clippety-clop come home again,' they said. Then they asked him: 'Which hedge have you been sleeping under?' And he answered: 'I did all right. Things would have gone badly if it hadn't been for me.' And they laughed harder than ever."

The king said to his daughter: "I shall proclaim a great festival, to last three days, and you'll toss a golden apple. Maybe the unknown knight will take part." When the festival was proclaimed, the youth went out to the forest and called Iron Hans. "What do you want?" he asked. "I want to catch the princess's golden apple." "You've as good as got it right now," said Iron Hans. "You'll have red armor for the occasion and ride a proud chestnut horse." When the day came, the youth came galloping into the courtyard and took his place among the knights. No one recognized him. The princess stepped forward and tossed a golden apple to the knights. He alone caught it, he and nobody else, but as soon as he had it he galloped away. The next day Iron Hans provided him with white armor and a white horse. Again he caught the apple and again he galloped away, without staying for so much as a moment. The king flew into a rage and said: "That's forbidden! He's obliged to appear before me and state his name." He gave orders that if the knight who had caught the apple should again run away, his men should pursue him, and strike him with their swords if he didn't come back of his own free will. The third day Iron Hans gave him black armor and a black horse, and again he caught the apple. But as he was galloping away, the king's men pursued him and one came so close as to wound his leg with the tip of his sword. Nevertheless, he escaped, but his horse reared so brusquely that his helmet fell off and his golden hair could be seen. The men rode back and told the king everything that had happened.

The next day the princess asked the gardener about his boy. "He's working in the garden. What a queer duck he is! He went to the festival and only came back yesterday evening. He showed the children three golden apples he had won." The king sent for the boy and when he came he was wearing his hat again. But the princess went up to him and took it off, his golden hair fell down over his shoulders, and it was so beautiful they all marveled. "Were you the knight," the king asked, "who came to the festival each day, each time in a different color, and caught the three golden apples?" "Yes," he said, "and here are the apples." He took them out of his pocket and handed them to the king. "If you wish for more proof, I'll show you the wound your men gave me when they were pursuing me. And I'm also the knight who helped you defeat your enemy." "If you can do such deeds, you're not a gardener's boy. Tell me: who is your father?" "My father is a mighty king, and I have plenty of gold, as much as I choose to ask for." "I see that I owe you a debt of gratitude," said the king. "Is there anything I can do for you?" "Yes," he said. "Indeed there is. You can give me your daughter for my wife." At that the princess laughed and said: "He doesn't beat about the bush! But I knew by his golden hair that he wasn't a gardener's boy." Whereupon she went over and kissed him. His father and mother came to the wedding, and they were very happy, for they had given up hope of ever seeing their beloved son again. And as they were sitting at the wedding board, the music suddenly fell silent, the doors opened, and a proud king came in with a great retinue. He went up to the youth, embraced him, and said: "I am Iron Hans. A spell turned me into a wild man, but you have set me free. All my treasures shall be yours."

The Three Languages

In Switzerland there was once an old count. He had an only son, who was stupid and couldn't learn a thing. The father said: "Listen, my son. I've tried and tried, but I can't drum anything into your head. You will have to go away. I'm sending you to a famous teacher; let him see what he can do with you." The boy was sent to a strange city, and spent a whole year with the teacher. Then he returned home, and his father asked him: "Well, my son, what have you learned?" "Father," he replied, "I've learned what dogs say when they bark." "Heaven help us!" the father cried. "Is that all you've learned? In that case I'll send you to another teacher in another city." The boy was brought to the second teacher, and again he stayed a whole year. When he returned home, his father asked him for the second time: "Well, my son, what have you learned?" "Father, I've learned what the birds say." The father flew into a rage. "Oh, you good-for-nothing!" he cried, "wasting all that precious time and learning nothing. Aren't you ashamed of yourself? Now I'm going to send you to a third teacher, but if you don't learn something this time, I won't be your father anymore." The son spent a year with the third teacher, and when he returned home his father asked him: "My son, what have you learned?" He replied: "Dear Father, this year I've learned what the frogs say when they croak." The father grew angrier than ever, jumped up, called all his servants, and said: "This dolt is no longer my son. I disown him. Take him out into the forest and kill him." They took him out into the forest, but when it came time to kill him they felt sorry for him and let him go. Then they cut a deer's eyes and tongue out and took them to the old count as proof that they had done his bidding.

The boy wandered from place to place. After a while he came to a castle and asked for a night's lodging. "Very well," said the lord of the castle. "If you are willing to spend the night in the old dungeon, you may stay, but I warn you, you will be facing great danger, for the place is full of wild dogs that bark and howl night and day. At certain hours a human must be brought in to them, and they devour him on the spot." Because of this the whole region lived in grief and sorrow, but no one knew what to do. The boy, however, was fearless. "Just give me some food for your barking dogs," he said, "and take me down to them. They won't hurt me." Since he himself insisted, they gave him food for the wild dogs and led him down into the dungeon. Instead of barking at him when he went in, the dogs gathered around him wagging their tails, ate what he set before them, and didn't harm a hair of his head. The next morning, to everyone's amazement, he came up safe and sound and said to the lord of the castle: "The dogs have told me in their language why they are living down there and bringing evil upon the country. They are under a spell and forced to guard a great treasure that is in the dungeon. They will know no peace until somone digs it up, and I have learned by listening to them how it can be done." All those who heard him were overjoyed, and the lord of the castle promised to

They gave him food for the wild dogs and led him down into the dungeon.

adopt him as his son if he performed the task. Down he went again, and since he knew what had to be done he was able to do it. He brought up a chest full of gold, and from that time on the howling of the wild dogs was never heard again. They had vanished, and the country was rid of them.

Some time later he took it into his head to go to Rome. On the way he rode past a marsh where some frogs sat croaking. He pricked up his ears, and when he heard what they were saying he grew thoughtful and sad. At length he arrived in Rome. The Pope had just died, and the cardinals couldn't make up their minds whom to choose as his successor. In the end they agreed to wait until God sent a sign. Just as this decision was announced—at that very moment—the young count entered the church, and suddenly two snow-white doves flew down on his shoulders and perched there. In this the cardinals saw a sign from heaven and asked him on the spot if he wanted to be Pope. At first he was undecided, for he didn't know if he was worthy, but the doves advised him to accept and at length he said, "Yes." He was anointed and consecrated, and thus was borne out the prophecy of the frogs that had upset him so in the course of his journey; namely, that he would become His Holiness, the Pope. Then he had to say a Mass. He didn't know a single word of it, but the two doves, who were still perched on his shoulders, whispered it all into his ears.

The Lilting, Leaping Lark

There was once a man who was going on a long journey, and as he was taking leave of his three daughters he asked them what he should bring them. The eldest asked for pearls and the second asked for diamonds, but the third said: "Father dear, I should like a lilting, leaping lark." "If I can find one, you shall have it," said the father, whereupon he kissed all three of them and started out. When the time came for him to return home, he had bought pearls and diamonds for the two eldest, but though he had looked everywhere, he hadn't found a lilting, leaping lark for the youngest, and that grieved him because she was his favorite child.

His way led him through a forest. In the middle of the forest there was a magnificent castle, and not far from the castle there was a tree, and in the very top of the tree he saw a lark lilting and leaping. "Oho!" he cried. "Well met!" He bade his servant climb the tree and catch the little bird, but as the servant approached, a lion, who had been lying under the tree, jumped up, shook himself, and roared so thunderously that the leaves on the trees trembled. "If anyone tries to steal my lilting, leaping lark," he cried, "I'll eat him up!" The man replied: "I didn't know the bird belonged to you. I'll gladly make amends and pay you good money if only you'll spare my life." The lion said: "Nothing can save you, unless you promise to give me

93

whatever creature you meet first when you get home; but if you promise me that, I shall not only spare your life but also give you the bird for your daughter." The man refused. "That could be my youngest daughter," he said. "It's she who loves me best and always runs to meet me when I come home." But the servant was afraid of the lion and said: "Maybe it won't be your daughter; it could just as well be a cat or a dog." The man let himself be won over, took the lilting, leaping lark, and promised to give the lion whatever creature he met first when he got home.

When he reached home and went into the house, the first creature he met was none other than his youngest, best-beloved daughter. She came running and hugged him and kissed him, and when she saw he had brought her a lilting, leaping lark she was beside herself with joy. But her father wasn't happy at all. He burst into tears and said: "Dearest child, this little bird has cost me dear. I had to promise you to a ferocious lion, and when he gets you he'll tear you to pieces and eat you up." Then he told her the whole story and implored her not to go, come what might. But she comforted him and said: "Dearest Father, if you've made a promise you must keep it. I'm sure I can calm the lion and return home safely." The next morning, after her father had shown her the way, she took her leave, and went fearlessly into the forest.

Now it so happened that this lion was an enchanted prince. He and all his courtiers were lions by day, but at night they resumed their natural human form. When she arrived, they welcomed her and took her to the castle. At nightfall the lion became a handsome man. The wedding was celebrated with splendor, and afterward they lived happily, staying up at night and sleeping in the daytime. One night he said to her: "There's to be a feast at your father's house tomorrow, for your eldest sister is being married. If you'd like to go,

So there the poor girl stood after traveling so far.

my lions will escort you." "Oh yes," she said. "I long to see my father." So she set out and the lions went with her. There was great rejoicing when she got home, for everyone thought the lion had torn her to pieces and that she had long been dead, but she told them what a handsome husband she had and how happy she was. She stayed there all through the wedding feast and then she went back to the forest. When the second daughter was to be married, she was again invited to the wedding. She said to the lion: "Don't make me go alone this time; I want you to come along." But the lion said that would be too dangerous, because if a ray of candlelight should strike him it would turn him into a dove and he would have to fly around with the doves for seven years. "Oh, please, please come!" she said. "I'll take good care of you and protect you from the light." So they went together and took their baby with them. When they arrived they arranged with the masons to build a room with walls so thick that no light could shine through them, and there he sat when the candles were lit for the wedding. But the door had been made of green wood that had dried and sprung a tiny crack that no one noticed. The wedding was celebrated with pomp and splendor, and when the procession with all its hundreds of torches and candles passed the room on its way back from the church, a hair's breadth of light fell on the prince, and the moment it touched him he was transformed. When she came in and looked for him, he was nowhere to be seen, there was only a white dove. The dove said to her: "For seven years I shall have to fly through the world. But every seven paces I shall let fall a drop of red blood and a white feather. They will show you the way, and if you follow my track you will be able to set me free."

The dove flew out the door and she followed it, and every seven paces a drop of red blood and a white feather fell and showed her the way. Farther and farther she went into the wide world. She never looked around her and never rested, and one day the seven years were almost over. Then she was happy, for she thought they would soon be set free, but they still had a long way to go. Once as she was walking along, no feather fell and no drop of blood, and when she looked up the dove had vanished. "No human being can help me now," she said to herself, and climbed up to the sun. "You shine on every hill and hollow," she said. "Have you seen a white dove by any chance?" "No," said the sun, "I haven't, but I'll give you a little box. Open it when you're in great trouble." She thanked the sun and went on until night fell and the moon came out. "You shine all night on every field and forest," she said to the moon. "Have you seen a white dove by any chance?" "No," said the moon, "I haven't. But I'll give you this egg. Break it when you're in great trouble." She thanked the moon and went on until the night wind arose and blew on her. "You blow over every tree and under every leaf," she said to the night wind. "Have you seen a white dove by any chance?" "No, I haven't," said the night wind, "but I'll ask the other three winds. Maybe they've seen the white dove."

The east wind and the west wind came and they had seen nothing, but the south wind said: "I have seen the white dove. It flew to the Red Sea, and there it became a lion again, for the seven years are over. The lion is fighting a dragon, and this dragon is an enchanted princess." And the night wind said to her: "I'll tell you what to do. Go to the Red Sea. On the right bank you'll see tall reeds growing. Count them, cut off the eleventh, and strike the dragon with it. Once you do that, the lion will be able to overpower the dragon, and both will regain their human form. Then look around and you will see the griffin on the shore of the Red Sea. Climb on its back with your dearest and it will carry you home across the sea. And now take this nut. When you're over the middle of the Red Sea, drop it. It will sprout, and a tall nut tree will spring up from the water for the griffin to rest on, because if it can't rest it won't have the strength to carry you across, and if you forget to drop the nut, it will let you fall into the sea."

So she went to the Red Sea and found everything just as the night wind had said. She counted the reeds on the bank and cut the eleventh and struck the dragon with it. The lion overpowered the dragon and both recovered their human form. But the moment the princess who had been the dragon was released from the enchantment, she picked the prince up in her arms, climbed on the griffin's back and carried him away with her. So there the poor girl stood after traveling so far, alone and forsaken again. She sat down and wept, but after a while she took heart and said: "I will keep going as far as the wind blows and as long as the cock crows, until I find him." Again she set out and traveled a long long way. Finally she came to a castle where he and the princess were living and heard they would soon be celebrating their wedding feast. She said to herself: "God will help me yet," and opened the little box the sun had given her. In it was a dress, as resplendent as the sun. She put on the dress and went to the castle, and all the courtiers and the bride herself looked at her with amazement. The bride liked the dress so much she thought it might do for her wedding dress. "Is it for sale?" she asked. "Not for silver and gold," the girl answered, "but for flesh and blood." The bride asked her what she meant by that, and she said: "Let me spend one night in the room where the bridegroom sleeps." The bride didn't want to let her, but she did want the dress, so she finally gave in, but she made the prince's manservant give him a sleeping potion. That night when the prince was asleep the girl was brought to his room. She sat down at his bedside and said: "I've followed you for seven years; I went to the sun and the moon and the four winds to ask after you, and I helped you in your fight with the dragon. Have you forgotten me entirely?" But the prince was sleeping so soundly that he only thought the fir trees

were sighing in the wind. At dawn they led her away and she had
to part with the golden dress.

When she saw her trick hadn't helped her, she was very sad. She
sat down in a meadow and wept, and as she was sitting there she
remembered the egg the moon had given her. She cracked it and out
came a mother hen and twelve little golden chicks, which ran about
and cheeped and crept back under their mother's wings. You couldn't
have imagined a prettier sight in the whole world. She stood up
and walked about the meadow, driving the hen and her brood before her until the bride looked out of the window and liked the little
chicks so much that she came down and asked if they were for sale.
"Not for silver and gold, but for flesh and blood. Let me spend another night in the room where the bridegroom sleeps." The bride
consented, planning to cheat her as she had the night before. But
when the prince went to bed, he asked his manservant about the
rustling and murmuring during the night. Then the manservant told
him the whole story, saying: "I was made to give you a sleeping potion because of a poor girl who secretly spent the night in your
room, and I'm supposed to give you another tonight." "Empty out
the potion beside my bed," said the prince. That night she was led
in again and when she began to tell him what a sad time she had
been having he instantly recognized his beloved wife by her voice.
He jumped up and cried: "Now I am really set free! It's as if I'd
been dreaming. The strange princess bewitched me and made me
forget you, but God has lifted the spell before it's too late."

They were afraid of the princess's father, who was a wizard, so
during the night they slipped away from the castle and climbed on the
griffin's back. The griffin carried them over the Red Sea. When they
were in the middle, she dropped the nut and a tall nut tree sprang up.
The griffin took a rest and then carried them home, where they found
their child, who had grown to be tall and handsome. After that they
lived happily until they died.

RALPH MANHEIM was born and grew up in New York. He graduated from Harvard College, studied at the Universities of Munich and Vienna and has, since then, translated books on a wide variety of subjects. In recent years he has specialized in fiction and plays. Mr. Manheim has won many awards for his translations of works by authors such as Günter Grass, Peter Handke, and Céline.

Mr. Manheim's deep-seated love for the Grimms' tales inspired him to undertake the prodigious task of translating from the German and compiling the first modern version of the complete tales. These were published together in his book GRIMMS' TALES FOR YOUNG AND OLD: THE COMPLETE STORIES. This remarkable translation has been heralded by *Publishers Weekly* as a "family treasure . . . [and] a labor of love by the internationally renowned translator and editor . . . It is a volume that transcends age barriers." *Library Journal* said, "Manheim has a wonderful ear, the tales are exciting to read aloud" and called Manheim's translation "the one truest to the magic of the original." It is from this prestigious collection that the fifteen tales in RARE TREASURES FROM GRIMM were selected.

ERIK BLEGVAD was born in Copenhagen, Denmark, and grew up in a family that loved art and artists. He studied at the School of Arts & Crafts in Copenhagen and has lived around the world in cities such as Paris, New York, and London. He is a well-known illustrator whose talented and sensitive drawings have appeared in many classic children's books and magazines.